RUNAWAY TRAIN

KATHY LEE

© Kathy Lee 2011
First published 2011
ISBN 978 1 84427 505 2

Scripture Union
207–209 Queensway, Bletchley, Milton Keynes, MK2 2EB
Email: info@scriptureunion.org.uk
Website: www.scriptureunion.org.uk

Scripture Union Australia
Locked Bag 2, Central Coast Business Centre, NSW 2252
Website: www.scriptureunion.org.au

Scripture Union USA
PO Box 987, Valley Forge, PA 19482
Website: www.scriptureunion.org

Scripture quotations are from the Contemporary English Version published by HarperCollins*Publishers* © 1991, 1992, 1995 American Bible Society.

British Library Cataloguing-in-Publication Data
A catalogue record of this book is available from the British Library.

Printed and bound by Nutech Print Services, India.

Cover design: Dodo Mammoth Reindeer Fox

Scripture Union is an international charity working with churches in more than 130 countries, providing resources to bring the good news of Jesus Christ to children, young people and families and to encourage them to develop spiritually through the Bible and prayer.

As well as our network of volunteers, staff and associates who run holidays, church-based events and school Christian groups, we produce a wide range of publications and support those who use our resources through training programmes.

Chapter 1:
Station Road

It was all Amy's fault. If it wasn't for Amy, I would have gone to football practice that Saturday morning. But Amy was ill again and Mum couldn't leave her.

"I'm sorry, Luke," said Mum. "I'll take you next week – I promise. But you know how it is…"

She had just made a promise she couldn't keep. But I was used to that. When Amy got ill, all promises were instantly forgotten.

I felt sick with disappointment. The football coach had told me that I might get picked for the next under-13 match, but if I didn't turn up to the practice session, I knew there was no chance.

"I could go on the bus," I said.

"Oh, is there a bus all the way to the football ground?"

"Yes. Number 38. I looked it up on the Internet."

This was a lie. I had no idea if I could get to the football ground by bus or not. I simply wanted to get out of the house, away from it all.

Normally, Mum would have wanted to know more details, but she couldn't spare any attention from Amy, who was about to throw up. I knew the signs.

"All right," she said. "Take some money out of my bag. And don't forget your mobile."

I went out without bothering to look for my football kit. She wouldn't notice.

Amy, my little sister, has cancer. It started when she was five, and they thought they'd managed to cure it. Now, three years later, it's come back. She's had chemo and radiotherapy; all her hair's fallen out, and her life is pretty miserable at the moment. But so is mine, and I can't even tell anyone. They would just think I'm totally selfish. After all, I'm not the one who might die before my next birthday.

I went down the road towards the middle of town. I thought I might hang out in the shopping centre, or maybe go to the bus station and find out about buses, for another time. Then I heard somebody calling my name.

It was Dylan Harvey, a boy from my year at school. He wasn't an actual friend of mine. Everyone thought he was a bit weird, obsessed with ancient myths and science fiction, and ghosts and things. But my real friends would be at football practice – Dylan was better than nothing.

"Where are you going?" he asked me.

"Nowhere special. You?"

Dylan looked secretive. But then, with his fringe of black hair half hiding his deep-set dark eyes, he often looked like that. "Do you really want to know?"

I said yes, although I didn't really care.

"I'm going ghost-hunting," he said mysteriously.

"I thought ghosts hung around at midnight, in graveyards and places. Not in Station Road at 10am."

"Oh yeah, like I'd be allowed to go out at midnight and wander round graveyards! I'm just going to look at this place that's supposed to be haunted. I want to see what it's like."

"Where is it?" I asked.

"The old railway line."

"What old railway line?" As far as I knew, Mallenford had never had a railway. But wait a minute – this road was called Station Road, so maybe long ago...

"Come and see," he said.

Because I had nothing much else to do, I went with him. If I could replay that scene, like a film flashback, I would scream at myself, *Don't do it!* But that never changes things in films, or in real life.

We came to an industrial estate between the town and the river. There was still no sign of a railway, but Dylan said that this was where the station used to be.

"Bit of a long way out of town," I said.

"That was down to the Earl of Mallenford. When the railway was being built, he didn't want it going anywhere near his house. He thought steam trains were filthy, noisy things. But nowadays people love them."

"How do you find out all this useless information, Dylan?"

"The Internet, mostly. And it's not useless – it's interesting."

"That's more than you can say for this place."

As it was Saturday, there wasn't much happening on the industrial estate. Most of the units were closed for the weekend, and some were closed for good, with boarded windows and *For Sale* signs. Rubbish had piled up like dirty snowdrifts against rusting wire fences.

"I wouldn't like to be here on my own at night," I said.

"You're not the only one. Night security staff never want to work here for long." He lowered his voice. "Sooner or later, they start hearing the trains."

"What? They hear trains on a line that doesn't exist any more?"

"That's what I mean about the railway being haunted."

I thought this was crazy. I could sort of understand the idea that people might come back as ghosts, to haunt places where they were unhappy in life or died a terrible death. (I didn't believe in ghosts myself. But I could understand why other people did... nobody wants to think that death is the end of everything.) But the ghost of a *train*?

"You're mad," I said. "The only ghost trains I believe in are the ones at fairs. And they're pretty useless... not even scary."

He paid no attention. He was unfolding an old, tattered map held together with Sellotape. He lined it up using the church steeple in the town centre and the monument on top of Mar Hill.

"I think this is about where the railway used to run," he said. "We must be right on top of it."

He drew a line in the air. In one direction was an empty car park. In the other, was a factory with a row of ice-cream vans outside. (So this was where ice-cream vans went in winter. They came here to hibernate until spring.)

There was no sign that there had ever been a railway here. But then Dylan pointed beyond the car park. "See that bridge? That's where it crossed the river."

We went closer to have a look. But we couldn't actually get onto the bridge. There were two iron gates, taller than a man, padlocked together. The gates were old, but the padlock and chain looked new and strong. Rusty coils of barbed wire ran along the top of the gates and down the sides of the bridge. An ancient, peeling sign warned: *Danger. Keep out.*

"What's dangerous about it?" I asked. The bridge still looked pretty solid, with six tall arches striding across the river. There were no railway lines or sleepers – they must have been removed when the line was closed down.

Dylan said, "I bet we could get past that barbed wire. All we need is some wire clippers – like in old movies where they cut their way out of prison camp."

"Why do you want to?" I asked him.

"I'd like to have a look at the tunnel. On the other side – see? It's marked on the map."

I looked across the river to where Mar Hill rose up, covered in thick woods. If there was a tunnel over there, it was quite invisible among the trees.

"The tunnel is where the accident happened," said Dylan. "Over 50 people were killed. That's what the monument is for, on the hilltop."

"I've never heard of it."

"But it's the only reason Mallenford is in the history books – the Mar Tunnel Disaster, 1869. Don't you know anything about your hometown?"

"It's not my hometown," I said. "I just live here."

We had come to live in Mallenford a year ago, when Mum and Dad split up. I still wasn't really used to it. I often dreamed about my old home, and in the dream, Dad had never left and Amy was well again. It was always horrible waking up.

"Mar Tunnel Disaster was one of the worst accidents in the early years of the railways," said Dylan. "A tragedy that should never have happened. It was all caused by a signalman making a mistake."

"So you think that's the reason for the haunting?"

He nodded. "The doomed train makes that journey time after time…"

"Do people actually see it?" I asked.

"No, they just hear it. You know what a steam train sounds like?"

"Of course I do." I made some Thomas the Tank Engine sound effects.

"You can't mistake that sound for anything, except a steam engine," said Dylan. "It couldn't be traffic noise or a low-flying plane, could it? So I don't know how else to explain what people have heard."

"Of course, they could be making the whole thing up," I said.

But in spite of myself, I was getting interested. I wanted to know more.

Chapter 2:

The base

"Come back to my place, if you like," said Dylan. "I'll show you what I know about the haunted railway. It's all on my computer."

"Okay."

I was actually quite curious to see where he lived. He was a bit of an odd character – maybe his house would be odd, too. A half-ruined mansion, full of ghosts, would be just right for Dylan.

But his house looked disappointingly normal. It was a red brick semi, with a tidy garden. We didn't go in; Dylan took me round the side towards what looked like a wooden shed.

"You keep your computer in the shed?" I said.

"It's not a shed," Dylan said, annoyed. "It's my base."

He unlocked the door, switched on a light and led me in. By now I'd guessed this wouldn't be anything like our shed at home, which was full of cobwebs and rusty gardening tools.

I was right. Dylan's base was more like a small room, with a computer desk, a chair and a square of carpet. There was a PlayStation, a shelf of books, a CD player... I looked around enviously.

"This is amazing," I said. "I wish I had a place like this."

"You should make yourself one then. I made this," he said proudly.

"What? All by yourself? I don't believe you."

"Well, Vince helped," he admitted. "All the ideas were mine, though. In summer I'm going to sleep out here. But it's a bit cold at the moment."

He turned on a fan heater. It blew hot air against my legs, without warming up the room much. Then he sat down in front of his computer. There was only one chair, so I had to perch on the edge of the desk.

Dylan did a search, found several websites which mentioned the railway accident, and chose one at random.

MAR TUNNEL RAIL CRASH, 1869

One of the worst railway accidents of Victorian times took place in the Mar Tunnel, north of Mallenford. A crowded train ran into the rear of another train in the depths of the tunnel. 56 people were killed and a further 82 injured.

The disaster appears to have been caused by signalling errors. In the early days of rail travel, there were no automatic signals; the trains were controlled by signalmen with flags.

The signalman at the south end of the tunnel, William Whittle, realised that two northbound trains were travelling too close together for safety (they should have been separated by a five-minute gap). He tried to stop the second train by waving a red flag, but did not think that the driver had seen his signal. The train disappeared into the tunnel.

Whittle could communicate by a telegraph wire to the signalman at the north end of the tunnel. He telegraphed, "Is train clear?" and received the message "Tunnel clear". Unfortunately, this referred to the first train, which had left the tunnel safely.

The driver of the second train had seen the red flag. He stopped his train inside the tunnel, waiting for instructions. Meanwhile, a third train was approaching. Whittle, thinking that all was safe, allowed it to enter the tunnel at normal speed.

Deep in the tunnel, it crashed into the rear of the second train, demolishing the guard's van and the last three carriages. Most of the deaths were in these carriages. The passengers were crushed to death, or scalded by steam from the engine's broken boiler.

"Nice way to die," said Dylan. "Crushed or scalded."

"At least it would be over quickly," I said.

"But you can see, can't you, why they might come back to haunt the railway that killed them?"

"Yeah, I can see why *people* might come back. If you believe in ghosts... which I don't. But how can you have the ghost of a train?"

Dylan said, "Oh, there are all kinds of stories about ghostly vehicles. A black coach and horses – the Earl of Mallenford's ghost is supposed to drive around in that. Or a ghost ship, like the *Flying Dutchman*."

"How come you don't get ghost cars and planes?"

"I bet they get a mention too. Let me look them up."

Sure enough, he found loads of references on the Internet, not only to ghost cars and planes, but ghostly motorbikes... cyclists... hitchhikers... anything we could think of.

"Ghost skateboarders?" I suggested.

"Don't be stupid," he said.

"Do you really believe in this stuff?"

"Not all of it," he said. "Half of what's on here is rubbish – urban myths... you know, it happened to somebody's brother's wife's cousin's best friend. Supposedly, but it's not *all* rubbish. It can't be."

"Why not?"

He said, "I've talked to a couple of people and recorded what they said. This is a guy from down the road, he used to work on the industrial estate. Have a listen."

He started playing a video clip on his computer. A man's face appeared on the screen. He looked about 40, going bald on top. He wore the dark uniform of a security guard.

"Interview with Charles Tucker, 21st January," came Dylan's voice, trying to be like an official reporter, but sounding more like what he was – a 12-year-old boy.

"Mr Tucker, you used to work on the Station Road estate on the outskirts of Mallenford. Can you tell me why you stopped working there?"

The man seemed to hesitate. "This is going to sound stupid, I know," he said. "But I was scared. I heard that train one night, and people say that if you hear it three times, you'll be dead within a year. So I quit."

"You heard a train on a railway that doesn't exist any more?"

"Yeah, that's right."

"Where were you at the time?"

"I was doing my regular check around the outside of the factory units. Must have been about midnight. It was pretty dark – no moon. Everything was dead quiet. And then…"

His voice faded, as if this was something he didn't like to talk about. Dylan prompted him: "And then you heard something?"

"Yeah. I heard like a train whistle, far away. And the sound of a train getting louder and louder."

"A steam train?"

"That's right. I never saw a thing, mind – I just heard the noise of it. It whistled again, the way a train would whistle outside a tunnel... and then the noise died away to nothing."

"Were you scared?"

"Of course I was! You'd have been scared too, son!"

"Did you run away?"

"No, but I spent the rest of that night indoors with all the lights on. And two days later I jacked the job in. I work at Tesco's now."

"Do you know anybody else who's heard the train?" asked Dylan.

"Yeah, one or two. Don't know if you'll get them to talk about it, though. It's supposed to be unlucky."

That was the end of the film clip. Dylan turned to me. "Well, what do you think? Was he making it up?"

I didn't know. The man had sounded quite convincing, but...

"Why would he make up something like that?" Dylan demanded. "Why would he be so scared that he left his job?"

"It is pretty strange," I admitted. "Did you talk to anybody else?"

"Yeah. This is Tom from next door." He played another clip, this time of a boy who looked about 16.

"... and don't mention my name," the boy said right at the start.

"All right, I won't," Dylan replied. "Interview with... er... a resident of Mallenford. Resident did not wish to be identified."

"Why not?" I asked Dylan.

"You'll see."

"And where were you when you heard the train?" Dylan's recorded voice went on.

"At the old watermill."

"Where is that, exactly?"

"By the river – not far from the railway bridge."

"Was anybody else with you?"

"Yeah, a couple of mates. We used to go there sometimes – nice and quiet, and the old Bill didn't bother us. I mean, it's not like we're doing anything that bad ... smoking weed, that's all ... having a drink or two."

"When was this?"

"Don't know exactly when – a few weeks ago. We were down there quite late one night. And then Ja..." He stopped himself from saying the whole name. (James? Jason? Jake?) "Like, one of the guys hears this noise. We don't believe him at first... he's kind of mental sometimes; he hears things that aren't there. But then we all hear it, and it's dead spooky..."

He went on to describe something very much like what the security guard had heard.

"There you go," Dylan said to me. "Two different witnesses. That would be pretty convincing in a law court."

"Shut up a minute." I wanted to hear the rest of the interview.

"We didn't hang around. We got out of there. And I've never been back."

"Do you think the haunting happens every night?" came Dylan's voice.

Tom shook his head. "That was the first time we ever heard it, and we'd been there quite a few times ... not going back to find out, though. No way."

The interview ended. I was actually quite impressed with Dylan's work.

"You could have a great career as a TV news reporter," I told him.

"That's exactly what I want to be – either that or an archaeologist."

"What, digging up old bones and things?"

"It would be interesting."

"*Interesting* must be your top favourite word, Dylan."

He thought about this. "I suppose it is. What's yours?"

"Football."

"Football's boring."

I didn't want to get into an argument about this. There are two kinds of people in the world, football haters (mostly female) and football fanatics. You can never change people's minds about it... I've tried. They are born like that.

I said, "What's that watermill place the guy was talking about? Ever been there?"

"No, but I'm going to have a look sometime," said Dylan.

"Tell me when you're going. I'll go too."

"We could go right now," Dylan suggested. "Are you up for it?"

Oh-oh. But I couldn't back out now, could I? "Yeah, all right," I said.

Chapter 3:
The old mill

"I just have to tell them I'm going out," said Dylan, and he went off indoors. A minute later he was back.

"Want something to eat before we go? June says she'll make us some bacon sarnies for lunch."

"Go on then."

We went into the kitchen. A grey-haired lady – June, I guessed – was already frying bacon, and the smell made my mouth water.

"Well, this is nice," she said, smiling at me. "It's not often that Dylan brings a friend home. Are you going to introduce us, Dylan?"

"His name's Luke," Dylan said, looking embarrassed.

"Hello, Luke. My name's June, and that's my husband, Vince, over there with his head in the paper."

Vince looked up and said hello. Unlike June, who was round and plump, Vince was lean, wiry and weather-beaten. I guessed they were both in their fifties.

"Are you in the same year as Dylan? Do you have the same horrible maths teacher?" June chatted away as she put the food on the table. In this house, people sat down at the table to eat, even if it was only a sandwich. There was a red checked tablecloth and a teapot with a knitted cover. It was all a bit old-fashioned, like an ancient sci-fi movie – the opening bit before the arrival of the aliens.

I wondered who June and Vince were. Obviously, they weren't Dylan's parents – they looked too old, and he called them by their first names. I wondered why he lived with them, instead of with his mum or dad.

"Where are you off to this afternoon, then?" June asked Dylan.

"Just exploring," said Dylan. That secretive look was on his face again.

"Whereabouts?" asked Vince.

"We thought we might take a look at the old watermill," I said. After all, what was the harm in letting them know that? But Dylan shot me an angry look.

"Oh, be careful," June said anxiously. "Don't go falling in the river. It's ever so deep around there. And the building is just a ruin, isn't it? Mind where you go."

Dylan totally ignored this. "Have you got a bike?" he asked me.

"Yeah, but it's no good. The chain's loose – it keeps coming off." That was something my dad could have fixed in a few minutes. But on the rare occasions when Dad came to see us, I never remembered to ask him.

"Bring it round, and I'll fix it for you," Vince offered.

"Yes, why don't you?" said Dylan. "We could ride to the mill then. It would be a lot quicker than walking."

So, after lunch, I ran back to my place and dug out my bike from the depths of the garage. Mum must have heard the crash as a stack of boxes fell over. She put her head around the door.

"Luke? Is that you?"

"No, it's a burglar nicking the flowerpots. Mum, I'm going out on a bike ride."

Mum didn't ask where I was going, or who with.

"Amy is asleep," she said, yawning. "I'm going to try and get some sleep myself while I can. I've got a feeling we might have a bad night."

"OK. See you later."

Vince fixed my bike chain, oiled it, and pumped up the tyres. As Dylan and I got ready to leave, June came out.

"Oh, be careful, boys. Remember how soon it gets dark, won't you? Be back before lighting-up time," she said.

Dylan looked annoyed again. He didn't say anything at the time, but as we set off, he said, "I wish June didn't worry so much. She's always fussing."

"You're lucky you have somebody to care about you," I muttered.

"What do you mean?"

I told him a bit about Amy and the way her illness was messing up my life. I hardly ever mentioned this to anyone. But somehow it was easy to talk, riding alongside Dylan. Maybe he really would make a good interviewer – he was great at getting people to open up.

But he wasn't so good at opening up himself. I asked him who June and Vince were, and he said coldly, "They're my foster parents. My real parents are dead."

"Oh."

As if to stop me asking anything more, he put on speed, overtaking me. By now we had left the town behind us. I followed him across a bridge and onto a narrow track along the riverside. On our right was the river, dark and deep. On our left was a steep, wooded hillside, with branches hanging over the path. The bare twigs clawed at my hair like skeleton fingers.

"Where is this mill place?" I asked.

"It can't be far now," Dylan said.

The valley and the river curved around. Now I could see the old railway bridge ahead. Before we reached it, the woods drew back a little, showing us the ruins of a building.

Not much was left of the mill. The roof and the windows had fallen in, and a rotting door hung open on broken hinges. Inside was a heap of rubble with a small tree growing out of it. A stone staircase went up one wall and stopped suddenly, going nowhere.

It would be a depressing place even in summer, I thought. On a grey winter afternoon, with a chill wind blowing through the gaps in the walls, it was almost scary. What must it be like after dark? No wonder people thought they heard strange noises.

"Someone's had a fire," I said, looking at the black, half-burnt sticks in a corner of the room.

"And a few drinks," said Dylan. There were empty lager cans here and there, and other rubbish – some of it pretty disgusting. "This must be where Tom and his mates used to hang out."

I said, "Why would they come here? It's horrible."

"You heard what he said on the video – people feel safe from the cops. A police car would never come down that track."

We looked around for a bit, finding what was left of the old waterwheel that used to power the mill. But that didn't interest Dylan just now. He had other things on his mind.

"I wonder if we could get to the railway tunnel from here," he said. "On the map, it doesn't look too far from the bridge."

Without even asking if I wanted to go, he set off towards the bridge. I followed him because I didn't want to be left at the mill on my own. It was creepy.

There was no path now. The woods came right down to the river's edge; we had to fight our way through the undergrowth. In summer it would probably be like the Amazon jungle, and even in winter a machete might have come in handy.

The bikes had been left behind at the mill. "Think they'll be safe?" I asked Dylan.

"Who's going to come here and nick them?" he said.

As we got closer to the railway bridge, Dylan headed up the hill at an angle. He was aiming for the place where the bridge met the land. We came to an iron fence, so old it was falling to pieces. There was an ancient, rusting metal sign: *Trespassers will be prosecuted. By order, Midland and Northern Railway.*

We walked straight past the fence and the sign. Nobody was watching us. No one would know or care that we'd been trespassing. The Midland and Northern Railway Company didn't exist any more, Dylan had said.

Battling through a mass of brambles, at last we reached the railway line – or rather, the place where the line had once been. On the far side of the river I could see the roofs of the industrial estate. On this side there was a cutting in the hillside, getting deeper as it went on, and curving round a corner out of sight.

"The tunnel must be just around there," said Dylan.

"The haunted tunnel," I said, feeling something shiver inside me.

"Yes, the haunted tunnel." He looked excited. "Come on, Luke. Not scared, are you?"

Chapter 4:
The thief

Dylan was right – it wasn't far from the bridge to the tunnel. Soon we could see the mouth of it – a stone archway at the far end of the cutting. I'd been wondering what I would do if Dylan suggested exploring inside it. Would I be brave enough to go with him?

But I needn't have worried. The entrance to the tunnel had been boarded up long ago, by the look of it. The boards were old, but still solid. There was a roughly-built door – locked, of course. Dylan rattled the handle and banged on the door.

I said, "You'd get a shock if it suddenly opened and a voice said, *Come in…*"

"Looks like somebody broke in sometime – or tried to." He pointed to a gash at the edge, with splintered wood showing pale against the dark door frame.

Why would people want to break into a tunnel? And why would other people try to stop them? There were two metal bars with padlocks holding the door tightly shut. They looked fairly new – still shiny, with no rust on them.

"Who do you reckon owns this place?" I asked.

"No idea. Like I said, the railway company went bust 50 years ago."

"If nobody owns it, who put those locks on the door?"

"The health and safety people, most likely," said Dylan. "It might be dangerous if kids wandered into the tunnel."

"Like us, you mean?"

"We're not kids. We are Investigators of the Paranormal," he said in a grand voice.

"You what?"

"The paranormal ... Ghosts and things ... Strange happenings that science can't explain."

He kicked the door a couple of times. Then he turned away. "This is a total waste of time. There's nothing to see – not in daytime, anyway. I wish I could come back here late at night."

"I don't. If you come back here at midnight, you're on your own, mate."

We fought our way back through the brambles towards the old mill. The winter daylight was fading fast. The ruined building was just a shadowy mound under the dark pine trees.

Suddenly, Dylan grabbed my arm. "There's somebody there! By our bikes!"

The person heard him. He looked round. Then he snatched up one of the bikes, jumped onto it and started riding away.

26

"Hey! Come back!"

My bike was the one that had been taken. Dylan leapt onto his bike and started racing after the thief. I ran behind, shouting.

It was useless, I thought – he had too much of a start. We would never catch him.

Then I heard a cry. The thief must have hit a pothole in the track. He'd gone right over the handlebars of the bike. He was lying at the side of the track, moaning in pain, and the bike lay beside him with its wheels still spinning.

Dylan skidded to a stop. A minute later, I caught up with him and grabbed my bike. We both stared at the boy who had taken it. He slowly stood up, rubbing his head. He looked about 16, with longish fair hair that could do with a wash. Actually, all of him could do with a wash – he was splattered with mud from his fall.

"I know him," Dylan said to me. "Jake Shipley. He's one of Tom's friends."

"What were you doing with my bike?" I said angrily.

The big boy stared me down. "I only took it for a laugh. Can't you take a joke?"

I didn't believe it had been a joke. I was pretty sure he'd been trying to steal the bike. But there was no point in arguing, for he was bigger and tougher than me.

"Come on," Dylan said to me. "Let's go."

"Wait. What are you doing here? Were you following me?" Jake demanded. He took hold of my handlebars so that I couldn't get moving.

I said, "No, of course not. Why would we want to follow you?"

"Because you're on their side."

"Whose side? What are you talking about?" I tried to twist the bike free, but I couldn't.

He leaned closer. His eyes were red-rimmed, with a crazy sort of look to them.

"You know who I'm talking about." He took a quick glance over his shoulder. "Don't let them fool you. They're evil. They can read your thoughts. If they catch you, they'll put a chip inside your brain and control you."

He was scaring me now. He must be mad, I thought. It was getting dark, and we were miles from anywhere with a raving lunatic for company.

Dylan got his mobile out. He said, "Leave my friend alone. Or I'll call the police."

Jake laughed. "Police? You think they're going to come down here?"

I looked at Dylan. Two of us together ought to be a match for Jake, but what if he had a knife on him?

All of a sudden, Jake's face changed. He let go of my bike and walked away, muttering something. He was heading towards the old mill. Dylan and I rode as fast as we could in the other direction. We didn't slow down until we reached the main road.

"Is there something wrong with that guy?" I asked Dylan. "He was acting really weird."

"I don't know. Maybe he just did it to spook us."

"No," I said. "It was like he really believed it. A chip inside your brain! He's a total nutter."

Dylan said, "I think he's the guy Tom was talking about on that video. *Kind of mental sometimes, hears things that aren't there* – that was what Tom said."

"The first one to hear the sound of the train."

"Yeah."

"So maybe he only thought he heard it, and the others were, like, influenced by what he said. Maybe there never was a ghostly train."

Dylan didn't want to believe this, I could tell. He said, "How do you explain the security guard, then? He was all on his own when he heard it."

"Don't know."

It was definitely getting dark now. The lights of the town were coming on, pale orange in the dusk.

"We'd better hurry," said Dylan. "June will be worried to death."

We rode across the bridge. The river, black as midnight, rippled under it, running down towards the ruined mill and the deserted railway bridge… and the crazy boy, Jake, alone there in the darkness.

★ ★ ★

I didn't get home until mid-evening. I'd eaten at Dylan's house – we had home-made chicken pie, the sort of thing Mum never had time to cook these days.

At home, Amy was looking a little bit brighter.

"Amy managed to eat some supper," Mum said. "Isn't that good?"

"Mum, I'm not a two-year-old," Amy said crossly.

I said, "Amy's a big girl now! Amy can count up to thirty-twelve!" (This was a family joke. Amy had actually said it when she was little.)

I sat down beside her on the bed. The living room was now Amy's bedroom, because she didn't have the energy to get up the stairs, and she was getting too big to be carried.

I didn't mind too much. If I wanted to watch the football, I had my own TV in my room. What I didn't like was the faint smell that was always in the room now, a smell of disinfectant and hospitals. Maybe it came from the chemical toilet in the corner – we didn't have a downstairs loo. Or maybe it was Amy herself. She'd spent so much time in and out of hospitals that she'd started to smell like them.

"Where have you been all day?" Amy asked me. So, while Mum was in the kitchen, I told her a little bit about Dylan and the ghost train. Her eyes went big and round.

"When I get better, can I come with you and look for ghosts?" she said. "But I'll need a new bike. That little pink one in the garage will be too small for me when I'm better."

"Yeah. When you're better." I patted her hand. In our house, nobody ever mentioned the fact that she might not get better. It hung over us like a dark cloud, like the coming of night. And we all ignored it as much as we could. Lovely weather we're having! Hope it lasts!

I went upstairs to watch Liverpool v Real Madrid. It was an exciting game, but before it finished, Mum came in.

"Luke, could I watch something on BBC2?" she asked me. "It's about a new cancer treatment they're trying out in America. I don't want Amy to see it because… well…"

I sighed and went downstairs. I knew Amy wouldn't want to watch the football. But it was all right – she'd fallen asleep with the TV still on.

Seeing her asleep, you wouldn't know there was anything wrong with her, apart from the silly little hat that covered her bald head. (She hated the wig that they'd given her; it was itchy, she said.) You couldn't see how weak and floppy she was. Mum said it wasn't the cancer that had done this to her – it was the treatment she was having.

Suddenly I felt angry. Why did people have to get ill? Why did families break up? Why did nothing go right in the world?

I changed channels. I'd missed seeing a vital goal being scored. But it didn't matter. My team lost in the end... I just knew they would.

Chapter 5:

The crossing

I didn't see much of Dylan at school. We were in the same year, but different forms, and Dylan never joined in the lunchtime football games.

Anyway, I had my own friends, who all thought Dylan was a bit strange. I didn't want them thinking I was strange too, so I never mentioned our "paranormal investigations". I did ask if anyone knew what had happened to Dylan's parents, but nobody could say.

On Friday evening, Dylan rang me.

"Are you doing anything tomorrow?"

"Football practice in the morning," I said. I was determined I wasn't going to miss it this week – I would cycle there if Mum couldn't take me.

"What about the afternoon?" asked Dylan. "Want to go on another bike ride?"

"Maybe. Where to?"

"Wait and see." He was being secretive again, and it annoyed me.

I said, "Let me guess. You want to go to the other end of that tunnel. But you said it yourself, it's pointless. There's nothing to see – not in daylight."

"I do want to see the far end of the tunnel, but there's something else as well. I saw it on the Internet – a haunted level crossing."

"What?"

"You know – a level crossing, where a road crosses the railway, not with a bridge or anything, just with gates."

"Dylan, I know what a level crossing is. But a *haunted* level crossing – that's stupid."

"Why is it any more stupid than a haunted tunnel?"

I had no answer to that.

Next day, after football practice, I rode round to Dylan's place. He showed me what he'd found on the Internet. It was on a website where people could post details of ghostly happenings.

A friend told me about this and I just had to see it for myself. It's a railway crossing near a place called Yanderton. People say it's haunted by the ghosts of some children who were killed when their school bus broke down there and got hit by a train. If a car stops on the crossing, it will be pushed clear of the tracks by unseen hands – by the ghosts of the children.

The crossing is on a quiet country lane between Yanderton and Hapchester. The road slopes slightly uphill. There are barriers that come down when a train is arriving.

We stopped the car on the crossing and my friend set up his video camera. With the engine in neutral, I took my foot off the brake. For a minute nothing happened. But then, very slowly, the car began to inch forwards. All by itself, it moved off the railway tracks – going uphill!

It scared me so much that, by instinct, I shoved my foot on the brake. The car stopped. But when I let go of the brake, it started moving again! It didn't stop until we were well clear of the crossing.

You don't believe me? Try it for yourself, or take a look at our video.

The video had been taken from the roadside. It certainly showed the car starting to roll forward, stopping, and then starting again.

"But that doesn't prove the car was moving on its own," I pointed out. "The driver could have been controlling it all the time."

"Yeah, I know," said Dylan. "That's why I want to take a look at the place."

"But we don't have a car."

"We've got our bikes. We could see if it works on bikes."

"Dylan, if you try to stay on a bike while it's not moving, something will happen, all right. You'll fall over."

"Oh, stop being so negative," Dylan said. "Are you up for it, or not? It's only 7 or 8 miles away. We could be there in less than an hour."

"Okay."

Just for a moment, I wondered if Mum would be happy to let me ride so far from home. But then there was no need for her to know, was there? I'd told her I was going on a bike ride with Dylan – she hadn't even asked who Dylan was.

At the moment, the only thing on her mind was that TV programme about cancer treatment. She'd watched it again when it was repeated. Then she started making phone calls. She was trying to find out if Amy could get help in America.

"If she does, it will be very expensive," Mum told me. "Medical treatment costs thousands of dollars over there. And then there would be fares, and hotel bills."

"Where would we get the money?" I asked. (Mum has a job as a translator, working at home, but it isn't very well paid.)

"Your dad might help," Mum said. She didn't sound too sure of this, because Dad kept telling us he was broke. The money he was supposed to send us always came late and sometimes didn't come at all.

"What if Dad can't afford it?"

"We'd have to borrow the money," said Mum. "Or even sell the house. It would be worth it, wouldn't it, if Amy got better?"

★ ★ ★

It was a cold day, but the sky was bright and clear as we set out. Dylan had told June we were going up Mar Hill, and he hadn't lied – the road out of town went over the hill. It was quite steep. We had to get off and push the bikes before we reached the top. But it was worth it for the long, swooping downhill ride, effortless as a bird.

A busy dual carriageway ran along the valley bottom. Before we reached it, Dylan said, "Stop a minute. That road isn't on my map."

He opened the old map. The dual carriageway didn't appear on it at all. The railway line was marked, and the tunnel.

"According to this," said Dylan, "the tunnel entrance should be down there, where the road is now."

You could clearly see the path of the old railway going out across the valley. It was overgrown with trees – a long, thin strip of woodland running across country. Foxes and badgers were probably living there now, with bird songs replacing the sound of trains.

The tunnel was invisible, buried under the banking of the new road. I thought Dylan would be disappointed, but he was more interested in finding his haunted railway crossing.

"That new road might actually be a short cut," he said.

"It looks terrible for cycling on," I said. "Look at all the traffic."

"There's a cycle path."

He was right – there was a cycle path marked out along the side of the busy road. But it must have been designed by a non-biker. It didn't feel wide enough to be safe. As we rode along it, the speeding cars seemed to be only a couple of feet away from my shoulder. And each time a truck went past, a gale-force wind went with it, trying to suck us into the road in front of the rushing traffic.

After what seemed like miles, we turned off the busy road, and I sighed with relief. There was another steep climb up to open moorland, where we stopped to eat the sandwiches June had made for us. Then the road dropped down into a valley. This was a much quieter road, with hardly any traffic. There was a railway, though. Now and then we heard a train hooting.

"My legs are getting tired," I complained.

"Mine aren't," Dylan said smugly.

"You didn't do football practice all morning."

"Football practice! I've got better things to do with my time."

We turned a corner and saw a level crossing ahead.

"Is that it?"

"I think so... if I read the map right. Come on!"

My legs suddenly found some new energy. The red and white striped barriers were open, standing on end.

Looking down the line both ways, we saw no sign of a train. We couldn't hear one, either. The only sound was the humming of wind in the wires above us.

A railway signal light shone green, as if to encourage us. We rode onto the crossing. There were two sets of tracks set into the tarmac, which was painted with criss-cross yellow lines. I knew what that meant – don't stop here. But we stopped.

"Isn't this a bit dangerous?" I said to Dylan.

"You are such a coward," he said impatiently. "Get off the track, if you're scared. I can try this on my own."

I told myself that it was perfectly safe. We would hear the train coming a mile off, and the crossing lights would flash. There would be plenty of time to get clear of the railway. Even if the barrier came down, we could easily go around the end of it.

Astride my bike, with one foot on the ground, I waited for something to happen. Was that the touch of a ghostly hand on my brow? No, more likely, it was just the wind.

"Nothing's happening," I muttered.

Dylan said, "Standing on the ground is like a car having the brakes on. Maybe if I get on properly…"

He managed to balance the bike for about two seconds before it began to topple over. Hastily he put his foot down again.

"What we'll have to do is start riding slowly, as slowly as we can without falling," said Dylan. "It's uphill, so that will help."

"And see if the ghosts give us a push?" I said, full of disbelief.

I copied him, getting on my bike and riding as slowly as I dared. But I'd only turned the pedals a couple of times when I felt it.

I was starting to speed up! Even though the road lay slightly uphill, the bike was moving faster than my slow pedalling. I stopped pedalling altogether, and still it gained speed! Unbelievable!

When I was about a hundred metres from the crossing, the movement slowed. The bike came to a stop, and I quickly got off. I looked at it nervously.

There was nothing odd about the bike. It looked totally normal. And yet it hadn't behaved normally. Weird!

"It really worked," said Dylan. His face was amazed. "I'm going to try it again."

"Me too."

We rode back towards the crossing. Although there was a slight downhill slope, somehow it felt like hard work. Was it because my legs were tired, or was it something else? Could it be that the ghosts wanted to keep us away from the crossing?

Suddenly, the warning lights began to flash red. An alarm bell started ringing – there must be a train coming. A minute later, the barrier closed, and we waited in front of it. There was a mournful hoot from down the line.

Soon the train went roaring past, with a rush of air and a thunder of swift wheels. It was twice as loud, ten times as powerful as the trucks on the main road. And I wondered what had happened when a train hit that bus full of children. It must have been totally demolished.

The train dwindled into the distance. The trackside signal changed from red to amber, to double amber, to green. But something was wrong with the barriers. They weren't opening up.

"Come on, come on," Dylan muttered under his breath.

A huge tractor arrived on the far side and stopped at the barrier. It had enormous wheels and a loudly growling engine. It was towing some kind of massive machine, armed with sharp-edged spirals of metal.

"Look at that," I said. "I've just thought of a new computer game – train v. tractor."

"The train would win every time," said Dylan. He was getting impatient. He hit the arm of the barrier. It shook, but stayed in place.

"The barrier isn't working," Dylan said. "But we can get round it. Look – there's nothing coming."

"No, wait," I said. "The lights are still flashing."

"You wait if you like. You could be there all day."

He wheeled his bike around the end of the barrier, turned it around and lined it up across the tracks. He got on; slowly he set it in motion. And then I heard it, faint above the roaring tractor engine... the hoot of a train.

"Dylan!" I screamed. "Get out of there!"

"There's nothing to worry about..."

Then he turned his head and saw it rushing towards him. I saw pure terror on his face. He leaned all his weight on the pedals... too late, I thought. Too late.

I shut my eyes.

Chapter 6:

The electric mile

I heard the train go roaring past. Slowly and fearfully I opened my eyes.

Dylan was quite close to me, clear of the barrier. He was still in one piece. He was smiling, but his face was white.

"Man, that was a close thing," he said. "I've never been so scared."

"Me, neither. I thought you'd be spread all over the tracks in a thin layer."

"Maybe the ghosts really did give me a push. What do you think?"

The red lights stopped flashing. The crossing barriers swung up. A man got down from the cab of the tractor and strode towards us. He looked absolutely furious.

"Just what do you think you're doing? This is a railway line, not a playground! You could have been killed, you little idiot!"

Dylan's smile faded. "We weren't playing," he said. "We were finding out about the ghosts."

"Oh, not again," the farmer said wearily. "I don't know who started that daft story, but people keep on coming, and I keep telling them – there are no ghosts

43

here. There never was a train crash at this crossing. But if this goes on, there soon will be!"

"There *are* ghosts," said Dylan. "I felt them – I really felt them pushing my bike up the hill."

"He's right," I said. "I felt it too."

The farmer said, "That was no ghost. Have you never heard of the force of gravity?"

"Gravity makes things move down, not up," Dylan said.

"Yes, and you were going down, not up. I know it doesn't look like it, but that's because of the way the land lies. The skyline isn't level. It's sloping downwards, steeper than the road, so the road looks like it's going upwards."

"An optical illusion, you mean," said Dylan.

"Are you sure?" I said. To my eyes, the road still seemed to be on an uphill slope. I couldn't make myself see it any other way.

He said, "When I was a lad, this bit of road was well known around here – the Electric Mile, people called it. They would put a football on the ground and watch it seem to roll uphill. How your story about ghosts started up, I've no idea."

"It's on the Internet," said Dylan. "Something about a train that crashed into a bus full of school kids."

The farmer snorted. "That never happened. Not here. I've lived within a mile of here for the last fifty years – I should know. But people keep on coming here and messing about on the crossing, like you did. One of these days there *will* be an accident, for sure."

Dylan looked as if he wanted to argue. I said hastily, "We'll keep off the railway. We know now how dangerous it is."

"Good. And why don't you tell them about this on the Internet? We don't want any more young idiots coming here, getting themselves killed."

"We'll tell them," I said. "We'll post a message on the website."

"They won't believe us," Dylan muttered.

At last the farmer calmed down and went back to his tractor. "Remember!" he shouted as he climbed in. "Keep off the crossing – you might not be so lucky the next time."

★ ★ ★

To cap it all, Dylan got a puncture on the way home. We tried to fix it using the repair kit in his saddlebag, but the patch wouldn't stick on properly. He would have to walk all the way home, pushing his bike. And it would soon be dark.

"I'll ring Vince," said Dylan. "If he's at home, I know he'll come and pick us up."

"What about the bikes?"

"We can put them in the back of his van. Just don't tell him what happened, all right? If you do, I won't be allowed to go on any more bike rides."

I heard him trying to tell Vince where we were, without giving too much away. "Yes, we did go up Mar Hill, but then we went on a bit further... we're in a lay-by on the road to Yanderton..."

We waited, getting colder and colder.

"I wish Vince would get a move on," said Dylan, shivering.

I said, "It's good of him to come and pick us up. I think they're really nice, Vince and June."

"Yeah," said Dylan. "They would adopt me if they were allowed to."

"Why aren't they allowed to?" I asked.

"Because my dad won't..." He stopped suddenly. Then he said, "Because my social worker says they're too old."

I wondered what he had been about to say. "Because my dad won't agree to it"? But hadn't he told me his parents were dead?

Maybe I would have asked him, but at that moment a van pulled up beside us. *Vincent Robertson, Carpenter*, it said on the side. Vince got out.

"Robertson's Breakdown Services and Bicycle Repair," he said. "Can I be of assistance?"

We loaded the bikes into the back of his van, on top of a heap of tools. Then we all squeezed into the front seat.

Vince said, "Did you have a good day? Before the puncture, I mean?"

"Not bad," said Dylan.

"I was always out on my bike when I was your age. But nowadays a lot of kids would rather sit in front of a computer. They ought to get out more. It's good healthy exercise, cycling."

He might not say that if he'd seen what happened to Dylan. Cycling had very nearly killed him.

"Did you live around here when you were young?" I asked him. "Did you ever hear of a road called the Electric Mile?"

"Oh, yes. I went there a couple of times. Funny feeling it gave you – as if you could go freewheeling up a hill."

Dylan said, "Wasn't there a bad railway accident around there a few years ago?"

"Not as far as I remember," said Vince.

"But I read about it on the Internet," said Dylan.

"You can't believe everything that's on the Internet, lad. There may be a lot of interesting stuff, but there's a lot of rubbish too. Nobody checks up on it, that's the trouble."

Dylan wasn't listening. When we got back, he went on the computer straight away.

"Look," he said. "That farmer man was wrong. There *was* a rail crash near Yanderton."

He had found a news report of an accident in 1978. A train had hit a bus which had stalled on a crossing.

Seven children were killed, and many others seriously injured.

"So it's not all made up," he said.

"Look again, Dylan. It happened near Yanderton, all right – Yanderton, South Carolina, USA."

"Oh."

He sounded let down. He had really wanted the story to be true. And so did lots of other people, by the look of it. The "haunted level crossing" story appeared on several different websites. Maybe it had started out as a simple mistake – now it had taken on a life of its own.

I said, "Vince was right. You can't believe everything you read on the Internet."

"No," said Dylan. "Pity."

Chapter 7:

Goodbye

Mum's endless phone calls were getting results. The American cancer specialist was willing to examine Amy, to see if the new treatment could help her. She would have to go to Boston for tests. If the treatment was suitable, she would stay there for six to eight weeks.

Mum would go with her, of course. I wanted to go too, but it would cost too much. We couldn't really afford the fares and hotel bills for two people, let alone three. Mum had borrowed a lot of money, partly by getting a bigger mortgage on the house.

"How will we ever pay it all back?" I asked.

"I don't know," she said. "Whatever it costs, it will be worth it, if only…"

I thought to myself: What if they couldn't do anything to help Amy? Maybe we would have to sell our house, and all for nothing. She would still die.

But I couldn't say that. I couldn't even put into words my feelings about being left behind. Mum had arranged that I would go and stay with Dad and Lynette in Nottingham. I wasn't too keen on Lynette, Dad's new partner, and I couldn't stand her two daughters. I'd spent a weekend with them once – that was more than enough. But eight weeks!

I started making my own plans.

"Mum, do I *have* to stay at Lynette's house?" I asked.

"If you were a few years older, you could stay here on your own. But you're too young, Luke. I'm really sorry you can't come with us. You won't be missing much, though. It's not a holiday – it'll be more like one long hospital visit."

"Why can't I stay in Mallenford with one of my friends?"

She frowned. "Eight weeks is an awfully long time to ask a friend to look after you. It's different with family."

"But Lynette isn't family," I pointed out. "She won't be too keen on me staying there, and her kids will absolutely *hate* it. Last time I went, the little one had to sleep in the big one's room, and the amount of fuss they both made, it was like they'd been sent to live in a rat-infested dungeon."

I knew that would make her smile. She didn't like Lynette any more than I did.

"Well, you could ask your friends and see what they say," she said.

At the start, I felt quite hopeful. But one by one, my friends – or rather their parents – said no. Callum's family of six didn't have the space for an extra one. Nathan's mum was waiting to have an operation. Ajit's family were going to India for a month. Alex's dad just said, No.

"And when I asked him why, he said, *Because*, and got annoyed with me," Alex reported. "Sorry, Luke. It would have been a real laugh."

Dylan was my last chance. I felt awkward asking him – it wasn't like we were real friends. But he seemed quite keen on the idea.

"I'll have to ask June and Vince," he said. "I bet they don't mind, though. They think you're doing me good – getting me away from the computer."

That very same evening, Mum got a phone call from June. They had a long chat, and when Mum put the phone down, she was smiling.

"Your friend's foster mum sounds lovely," she said. "She said what a nice young man Luke is, always so well-behaved. I thought, are we talking about the same person?"

"So can I stay with them?" I asked eagerly.

"Yes. I expect Lynette will heave a big sigh of relief."

"Me too."

A fortnight later, I moved a lot of my things to Dylan's house. A few days after that, I went to the airport to wave Mum and Amy off. Dad was there too. He gave Amy a fat purple teddy bear, which I could see she wasn't keen on. She would probably manage to lose it somewhere in America.

I hugged her, rather awkwardly because she was in a wheelchair.

"Don't eat too many burgers," I told her. "Don't drink too much Coke."

"I really, really hope I'm not sick on the plane," she said. Her face was pale.

I whispered, "You could always be sick on that teddy," and she giggled.

We said our goodbyes. Mum pushed the wheelchair towards the departure area. One last wave – then they were gone.

★ ★ ★

Dad drove me back to Dylan's house. He was rather quiet on the journey. After a while I realised what the trouble was… He was upset because I hadn't wanted to go and stay with him.

"Dad, if it was just you, I'd love to stay at your place," I said. "But Lynette's always there, and her kids."

"Well, it is their house. Maybe I shouldn't have moved in there. I should have held onto that flat I was renting – at least I had my own space."

"Not much of it," I said, because the rented flat had been very small. A sofa bed, a cooker, a fridge, a tiny shower room – all squeezed into a space not much bigger than our kitchen. "There wouldn't even have been room for me to kip on the floor there."

He sighed. "And it was costing me an arm and a leg."

I said, "Dad, do you ever wish you could turn back time? Go back to a time when you were happy, and stay there?"

He didn't give me a straight answer. He said, "What time would you choose to go back to, then?"

"To before Amy got ill." *Before you and Mum split up,* was what I really meant.

"Yeah, that would be nice. But we can't. Things change, son. We can't go back."

I knew what he was trying to tell me. He was never going to get back with Mum, so I needn't waste my time hoping for it.

He dropped me off at Dylan's place. June offered him some tea, but he was in a hurry to get back to Nottingham. I said goodbye, and he drove away.

When he was gone, I went upstairs to my new bedroom. I lay on the unfamiliar bed, feeling suddenly homesick. Stupid! I hadn't even been away from home for one night yet!

Somehow June must have guessed how I might feel. She'd cooked a chicken pie because she knew I liked it. After supper she dug out an ancient Monopoly set, and all four of us had a game. Dylan won, but it was close. June lost by a mile – she was too kind, letting people off all the time.

Before bedtime, Mum rang to say they'd arrived safely, but Amy was very tired. She'd already gone to bed, although it was only three o'clock in Boston. She would have Sunday to recover from the flight, and the doctor would see her on Monday.

"Are you all right, Luke?" Mum asked me from the other side of the Atlantic.

"Of course I am. Don't worry about me, Mum. I'll be fine. Just fine."

★ ★ ★

Next morning I got a bit of a shock. June and Vince asked if I would like to go to church with them.

Church! I hadn't been to church since Mum took us to a Christmas service about three years before. *No thanks*, I wanted to say. I just knew it would be boring.

"Is Dylan going too?" I asked.

"He usually does. But you don't have to if you'd rather not. We'll only be out for an hour or so."

"All right, I will," I found myself saying.

When I got Dylan on his own, I said, "I never knew you were religious."

"I'm not," he said. "I don't really believe in God."

"Then I don't see why you go to church."

"June likes me to go. Anyway, it's sometimes interesting – the paranormal side of it. I saw a guy getting prayed for once, and he suddenly fell over and just lay there. It was weird. And another time, when Vince had a bad back, they prayed for him and it got better, just like that. There must be... I dunno... some kind of special power when people get together and pray about something."

"Do you have to be in church to get prayed for?" I asked. "Or can it work if you're far away?"

"I think so. You mean your sister?"

"Yes."

"Ask Vince or June. They'll know."

When I asked June, she said she was already praying for Amy every day. If I wanted it, her name could be put on the prayer list at church, so that lots of other people would pray for her, too.

The church service was another surprise. It wasn't in an ancient building with stained-glass windows and wooden pews. It was held in a junior school hall, smelling of floor polish and school dinners. Instead of droning organ music, there were noisy songs to the sound of guitars and drums. This couldn't really be a proper church, I decided. But at least it wasn't boring.

At the end, the man in charge said that if anyone wanted to be prayed for, they should go to the front of the room. Feeling rather nervous, I asked June to go with me. I told the man about Amy, and he prayed for her. It was strange the way he prayed – not in a posh voice with lots of long words, more as if he was talking to a friend.

Afterwards, for some reason, I felt a bit better about Amy. I had done what I could for her. Maybe it wouldn't make any difference at all – but at least I'd tried.

Chapter 8:

Brothers

On Monday night, the news was good. The American specialist had agreed to put Amy on his treatment programme.

"He said we mustn't get our hopes up too much, though," Mum told me. "This medicine doesn't work for everybody. Some people get bad side effects and have to stop using it. But others…"

"Others get better?" I said.

"Yes."

When I told June this, she said, "We must keep on praying. Every time you think of Amy, you can send up a prayer for her. And I will, too."

So I often prayed to the God I didn't believe in. *If I'm wrong, God… if you do exist… please listen to me. Please let Amy get well again.*

By now I was beginning to feel at home in Dylan's house. Actually, in some ways, it was better than being at home – the food, for one thing. June loved to cook, and unlike Mum, she had the time to do it. She never bought frozen pizzas or microwavable meals. (Just as well, since she didn't own a microwave.) Her home-made pizzas were wonderful. Her chocolate cake was the nicest I'd ever tasted.

June and Vince were a bit old-fashioned. They wouldn't let us watch some TV programmes. They hated what June called "bad language". They liked things to be neat and tidy, and they ate at the same time every day. It was rather like living with grandparents, instead of parents. But I didn't mind that. I missed my grandparents... I had only seen Dad's parents once since Dad and Mum split up.

The thing that had really worried me was: Would I get on all right with Dylan? He could be annoying sometimes. Would he want to go off on crazy ghost-hunting trips all the time?

But so far we were getting on fine. We had separate bedrooms, so we each had our own space. And there was Dylan's base, too, if we wanted to play computer games, or just chill out. It was almost like having a brother – I always used to wish I had a brother to hang out with.

One day, after school, we were in the base watching music videos.

"Maybe we could sleep here overnight," Dylan said. "It would be cool. Almost like camping."

"Cool? Freezing cold, more like," I said.

"Not if we had sleeping bags. Hey... I just had a great idea."

He wouldn't tell me what the idea was. "Wait and see," he said, annoying me again.

"I've had a great idea too," I said. "If you go along with it, I promise to go along with your idea, whatever it is."

"Okay then."

"My idea is, you learn to play football."

"Football!" Dylan groaned. "It's so boring. And I'm useless at it."

"You're useless because you never play. If you practise a bit, you'll definitely get better at it. Why don't we go and have a kick-around in the park?"

So we took my football to the small park at the end of the road. I showed Dylan some of the techniques I'd learned at football practice. Then we took turns at shooting and defending the goal. Although his kicking wasn't great, Dylan was surprisingly good at goal-keeping.

"Where did you learn to catch and throw like that?" I asked him.

"My dad used to teach me. He liked basketball and cricket, not football." This was only the second time Dylan had ever mentioned his dad.

"How old were you when he died?" I asked, curious.

Dylan pretended he hadn't heard me. He dropped the ball and kicked it hard. It landed in some thick bushes at the edge of the park. When we found it again, it was starting to deflate, so that was the end of the football session.

As I came out of the bushes, I saw someone I recognised. Instantly I ducked down.

"It's that crazy guy," I whispered to Dylan. "Keep down – don't let him see us. He'll think we're following him again."

Jake went slowly towards a wooden shelter near the swings. His shoulders were hunched; his head was down. A couple of times he looked around in a suspicious kind of way, but he didn't notice us.

Suddenly I heard a rustling in the bushes quite close to us. A young boy – about 9 or 10 years old, I guessed – came creeping along next to the fence. He looked startled when he saw us.

"Are you after him too?" he said.

We stared at him blankly. "After who?" said Dylan.

"Jake. My brother."

"Of course not," I said. "We're playing football."

"What, in the bushes?" the boy said, disbelieving. "Looks to me like you're spying on him. Has he nicked something of yours?"

"He tried to take my bike once," I said. "If you really want to know, the reason we're hiding here is to keep away from him."

The boy looked angry. "I wish I could keep away from him. I wish my mum had the guts to kick him out! I hate him!"

"What's he done to you?" Dylan asked.

"He's always moody and horrible. And he nicks things. Today he took £20 that I got for my birthday – I want to get it back."

"How are you going to do that?" said Dylan.

"I don't know. He's bigger than me, and when he gets angry, it's scary. He punched a hole in the door last week. It's not fair! Nothing's safe in our house! I really hate him. I wish he was dead."

I felt sorry for the boy. "You should tell somebody. Tell your mum what's going on."

"What can *she* do?" he said scornfully. "When he gets angry, she's scared of him too. She says it's because he smokes too much weed. She's tried to get him to stop. But he won't."

"I suppose that's why he steals things," said Dylan. "To pay for the weed."

I said, "And it looks like his next delivery is on its way. There's Tyson's car."

Tyson was a man who was often around as we came out of school. When boys in our year headed towards the ice-cream van, older boys made for Tyson's car. Now it had pulled up outside the park gate, and Jake hurried towards it. For a minute I thought his brother was about to run after him, but he chickened out.

We watched as Jake came back from the car. He went into the shelter again, and soon we saw the red glow as he lit up. I caught a faint whiff of the smell that sometimes hung around the bike sheds at school.

"Tom, next door, says it's harmless," said Dylan. "Smoking weed, I mean. He says he'll let me try it sometime."

"Dylan! June would have a fit if she heard that."

He said, "Maybe it is okay, though, if you only smoke it now and then. It doesn't seem to have done Tom any harm."

"It's harmed my brother," the young boy said bitterly. "It's doing his head in. He like hears voices that aren't there. He says he keeps hearing his name on TV. He never used to be like this before he started getting stoned."

Dylan began to laugh to himself.

"What's so funny?" Jake's brother demanded.

"When Jake told us about people following him, we thought he was a complete nutter. But somebody *is* following him – you. Perhaps he's not quite as crazy as he seems."

"He is crazy. And he's driving my family crazy too," said the boy. "I hate him! I wish he'd never been born!"

Maybe it wouldn't be so great having a brother, I decided. Friends were better because you could choose them. With family, you had no choice. Whatever they were like – good or bad, sick or healthy, loving or hateful – you were stuck with them.

Chapter 9:
Health risks

Vince and June had a grown-up daughter who lived in London. The next weekend it would be Vince's birthday, so she was coming home for a couple of days. I was sleeping in what used to be her bedroom – I would have to move out. I said I didn't mind sleeping on the sofa or on Dylan's bedroom floor, but Dylan had other plans.

"We could both sleep in the base," he said.

"Oh, dear. Do you think you'll be warm enough?" June said.

"We can come indoors if we really start shivering," said Dylan. "It's not like we'll be camping in a field somewhere."

I couldn't understand why he was so keen to do this. But when we were on our own, he told me.

"Remember I said I'd had an idea? And you said you'd go along with it, if I played football with you?"

"Yes," I said cautiously, wondering what I had let myself in for.

"Well, if we sleep out here, we can easily get out in the middle of the night. We can go and look for the ghost train."

"Oh, no," I said. "No way."

"Come on, Luke. Just once, that's all I'm asking. It's the only way we're ever going to find out more."

"I don't want to find out more," I said. "That old mill was scary enough in daylight, never mind at night."

"I'm not talking about the mill. I was thinking of going to the industrial estate. Perfectly safe. There are street lights and everything."

I still didn't like the idea. "You go, then, if you're so keen."

"Not on my own," he said. Maybe he wasn't as brave as he liked to pretend.

He tried a different approach – bribery. "Listen, if you come with me, I'll play football as much as you want for a week."

"For a whole week?"

"Yeah. Deal?"

"Deal."

I told myself that there was nothing to be scared of. From what we'd heard, the ghost train didn't make its journey every night – only now and then. Most likely we wouldn't hear anything at all.

* * *

Vince and June's daughter, Laura, arrived on Friday evening. She wasn't at all like I had expected. She had stylish clothes and fashionable short-cropped hair, and she drove a bright red Mini. She worked in advertising.

When we watched TV, she found the adverts more interesting than the programmes.

"That's one of ours," she said about an ad for pasta sauce. "We tried to get what's-his-face, that TV chef, but he cost too much. Good thing really. It was just before the Health and Safety people shut down his restaurant."

"Do you mind if I switch over now, dear?" said June. "There's something I would like the boys to see on the other side. I read about it in the paper."

The programme she wanted us to see was about drugs – cannabis, mainly. At first it was pretty boring stuff that we'd already learned at school. But then it focussed on one boy. He was 15 and he often smoked cannabis. His mother said it made him moody and sometimes violent. If she tried to make him get out of bed and go to school, he got very angry. One day, when she wouldn't give him any money, he hit her so hard that she ended up in hospital.

Dylan and I exchanged glances. "Remind you of anybody?" said Dylan.

A psychiatrist was interviewed. She said, "People think that cannabis smoking is pretty harmless. And for many people, that's true. But for some – a minority – it appears to cause serious mental health problems. If you start smoking cannabis heavily at a young age, you may increase your chances of becoming mentally ill."

"Oh, really," said Laura. "How ridiculous! They do like to frighten people, don't they?"

"Would you say it's all right to smoke weed, then?" asked Dylan. "Have you tried it?"

"Of course I have," said Laura. "Anybody my age who says they've never touched it is probably lying. Don't look so shocked, Mum. It hasn't turned me into a raving psycho."

"Girls, girls. Can you argue somewhere else, please?" said Vince. "Some of us are trying to watch this."

The programme was now showing a city at night, filmed from the air. One house roof showed up very plainly on the infra-red camera. It was giving out far more heat than its neighbours.

"When police raided this house, they found a secret cannabis factory. Every room was full of cannabis plants, growing in artificial light and heat. Under these conditions a new crop can be produced several times a year, with a street value of £50,000 to £100,000 each time. Dozens of similar factories have been raided in the last year. Many more may still be operating undetected.

"This type of cannabis can be far more potent than the old variety. Its effects are stronger. More and more people are smoking it, starting at a younger age than ever before. In our survey, over 40 per cent of 15-year-olds had tried it."

"Yeah," said Laura, "and I bet 90 per cent of them have tried alcohol. That's what the real problem is, if you ask me. Alcohol must kill far more people than cannabis. They get in fights, they drive when they're over the limit... "

"Laura," her mother said in a warning voice. She was talking to Laura, but her eyes were on Dylan.

"This girl I know," Laura went on, "she let her boyfriend drive her home when he'd had a few, and..."

"Laura! Come here a minute. I want a word with you," said Vince.

They went out into the kitchen. June was still looking anxiously at Dylan. He seemed to be engrossed in the TV.

When Laura came back in, she was unusually silent. We watched the programme to the end, and then June said it was bedtime. (This was one of the drawbacks of living at Dylan's house. Bedtime was strictly 9pm.)

It was pouring with rain as we went out to the base. Excellent, I thought. Even Dylan wouldn't want to go ghost-hunting in a downpour.

Vince had dug out two ancient camp beds from the attic. June had found us sleeping-bags and pillows. The heater had been on for a while, and the base actually felt quite cosy. We lay in the darkness, listening to the rain drumming on the roof.

"What was all that about, indoors?" I asked Dylan.

"All what?"

"You know. Vince hauling Laura out of the room for a secret confab."

"I suppose it was because of me," he said.

"What do you mean?"

"I guess you had to find out sometime." In the dark, I couldn't see his face. His voice sounded cold and flat. "When I was nine, we went to a wedding, and my dad had a lot to drink. Mum was supposed to be driving home, but Dad wouldn't let her. He said he could drive better than her any day, drunk or sober."

Oh-oh. I could guess what was coming next.

"He was driving too fast. She was telling him to slow down. We came round a corner and there was this car that had stopped in the road. Dad couldn't brake in time."

There was a silence. I could not think of a single word to say.

Dylan said, "Two kids in the other car got killed. My mum... my mum died too. My dad went to prison. I ended up in care. There – now you know."

Chapter 10:
Tonight's the night

I wanted to tell him that I understood. I knew why he'd told me his parents were dead, even though his dad was still alive. I understood why he wanted to find out if ghosts really existed.

But the words dried up in my throat. How could anyone really understand what it felt like? Dylan's father had caused his mother's death, and put Dylan's life at risk too. All because he'd had too much to drink and was too stubborn to admit it.

My own problems were tiny compared with Dylan's. My sister was ill and my family had split up... so? Dylan's family hadn't just split, it had been smashed to pieces.

The empty silence stretched out longer and longer. Desperately trying to find something to say, I asked him, "Is your dad still in prison?"

"Yes, and I don't care if he stays there for the rest of his life," said Dylan. "I hate him. It's all his fault, this – all of it."

"It was an accident, though," I said. "He didn't mean to do it."

"Wasn't an accident when he kept knocking back the drink, though, was it? Wasn't an accident when he wouldn't let Mum have the car keys. Or when he drove too fast. He chose to do all that."

Now his voice was full of anger and pain. I really hoped he wasn't about to cry. I didn't know how to cope with that.

"I hate him!" Dylan said fiercely. "I wish he'd died instead of her!"

"I don't blame you," I said.

Neither of us spoke after that. The heater whirred endlessly; the rain pattered on the roof. The night was like a dark, unending tunnel. I couldn't get to sleep for ages.

★ ★ ★

The next day, Dylan didn't even mention what we had talked about. He seemed to be back to normal, and I felt relieved.

It was Saturday, Vince's birthday. Dylan gave him a giant bar of Toblerone. June had bought him a book and cooked his favourite meal. Laura took him into town to choose a new jumper. I felt left out, with nothing to give him. (Mum had forgotten to leave me any pocket money when she went away.)

I said to June, "I wish I could get Vince a present. But I've got no money."

"If you like, you could give him a really good present," said June. "And it wouldn't cost you anything except your time."

"What do you mean?"

"Clean his van for him. It's filthy."

This was true. The weather had been bad, and now the white van was mostly dark grey, except where somebody had scribbled a message on the back: *Also available in white.*

With Dylan's help, using a hose fixed to an outside tap, I gave the van an extra good clean. Even the hubcaps were sparkling. When Vince came back, he got quite a shock.

"The old van hasn't looked this good in years," he said. "Thanks, lads."

I felt pleased. I liked Vince – he was as nice as June, but he didn't worry as much. He could remember what it was like to be young. He liked to talk about the things he used to do at our age – fishing, camping out in the woods, and cycling for miles. It seemed as if boys had more freedom in those days.

"Of course, there wasn't so much traffic on the roads then," he said.

"And things felt safer, somehow," June said. "You didn't hear so much about violence and crime."

Laura laughed. "Violence and crime? In Mallenford? Mum, you should be glad you don't live in Hackney."

"When you went camping," Dylan said to Vince, "did you go into the woods on the far side of the river?"

Vince shook his head. "Those woods were used for pheasant-shooting when I was a lad, and the gamekeeper would give you a thrashing if he caught you."

"Was the railway line still running in those days?" Dylan asked.

"No, it had shut down before I was born."

"Did you ever hear anything about the railway being haunted?" I asked him.

"Only the daft kind of things that boys say to scare each other," said Vince. "Sitting round a fire in the dark, you'll believe anything. Load of nonsense really. We'd hear the wind in the trees and think it was the old Earl riding by with his coach and his black horses!"

"But the train. Did you ever hear the sound of a train?"

"No. My friend said he heard it once, but I didn't believe him. It's just a story, son."

"Don't you go worrying about ghosts," said June. "There's no such thing."

She didn't understand. She didn't realise that Dylan *wanted* to believe in ghosts – wanted to know that people could live on after death. And he wasn't the only one. If Amy died, would she disappear forever? Or would some part of her still exist somewhere?

I said, "What do you think happens to people when they die?"

Vince said, "It says in the Bible that if you believe in Jesus, you'll go on living after you die. You'll live forever in heaven. Do you want to know what it will be like?"

He got a Bible from the bookshelf, opened it, and started reading aloud.

> God will live with them, and they will be his people. God will wipe every tear from their eyes, and there will be no more death or sorrow or crying or pain. All these things are gone forever.

"And this is what Jesus said about heaven," Vince went on, turning to another part of the book.

> Trust in God, and trust also in me. There is more than enough room in my Father's home... I am going to prepare a place for you.

For some reason, I liked the sound of these words. But I could see that Dylan didn't. Maybe it was the word *Father* that made his face look cold and hard, like a marble statue.

"If we trust in God, death isn't something to be scared of," said June. "We know that we're going to meet him when we die. We'll live in his house. We'll see him face to face."

Trust in God… what did that mean? How could you trust somebody you'd never met – someone who probably didn't exist?

I wanted to ask this, but I didn't get the chance. My phone rang. It was Mum, giving me the latest update on Amy. Although it was too soon to know if the treatment was helping her, Mum said she was feeling all right. The new medicine didn't seem to make her sick like the one she had before.

"Can I talk to her?" I said.

We chatted for a short while. Amy said she liked the American hospital because it was like the ones on TV.

"What, full of emergencies?"

"No, full of Americans. And I met this girl, she's really nice. She's called Brooke and she comes from Chicago. She said she just *adores* my accent."

"Maybe you won't want to come back to boring old Britain," I said.

"Don't be silly," said Amy. "Are you all right, Luke? What have you been doing?"

"Oh, the usual," I said.

"Are you going on any more ghost hunts?"

"Yes, but I can't talk now. I'll tell you all about it when you come back."

Not long after, it was bedtime. Dylan and I went out to the base. The night was very cloudy, without a star to be seen. But there was no rain – much to my disappointment.

"Tonight's the night," Dylan whispered. "We wait till all the lights go out. Then we make a break for it."

"You make it sound like the *Great Escape* or something," I said, "like we're going to get machine-gunned by the guards."

Dylan laughed. "I can't imagine June or Vince letting loose with a machine-gun."

"They wouldn't exactly be pleased, though, if they knew what we were doing," I said uneasily.

"Not going to know, are they? Come on now. Lie down and pretend to be asleep."

I pretended so well that soon I was asleep. Not for long, though. A sudden, earthquake-like movement tipped me sideways off the camp bed. And out of the earthquake came a voice.

"Wake up, Luke," said Dylan. "We had a deal, remember? We're going ghost-hunting."

Chapter 11:

Sounds in the night

It was 20 minutes to midnight. I crawled out of my sleeping bag, rubbing my eyes and wishing I hadn't agreed to go on this stupid ghost hunt.

"Shhh," said Dylan. "We have to be really quiet. I think Laura's still up – the kitchen light's on."

"Then why don't we wait until she's gone to bed?"

"That might not be till 2am. And midnight is the best time for ghosts."

"Oh, all right. May as well get it over with."

As quietly as we could, we crept round the back of the base to where the bikes were kept. Then we had our first setback. My front tyre was as flat and soft as a fried egg.

I thought this might change Dylan's mind, but he whispered, "We'll walk, then. It's not that far."

"We won't get there before midnight," I said.

"We will if we hurry."

Silent as shadows, we slipped down the side of the house and out through the front gate. The street was deserted. In most of the houses the lights were off. The only things moving were a couple of cats, out on their own night's hunting.

It was a chilly night. The sky was covered in thick, dark clouds, lit with an eerie glow by the lights of the town.

"Hurry up," Dylan whispered.

"I am hurrying. Why are you whispering?"

"Don't know," he said. "I've never been out this late on my own. It feels spooky."

"We can go back, if you like," I said hopefully.

"No way. Not now we've got this far."

We didn't go through the town centre. Dylan said there might be too many people about. He led me around the outskirts of the town, through quiet roads where we saw hardly anyone. At last we reached the edge of the industrial estate. But we couldn't get in – there was a high fence, topped with barbed wire.

"It *is* like the *Great Escape*," I said. "Where are the guards?"

"That's a point. There probably is a security guy somewhere about. We'll just have to be careful."

"Why? We're not breaking the law."

"No, but I bet we look as if we're up to something. Kids our age, out this late – people get suspicious."

Faintly on the wind came the sound of a church clock striking midnight. I counted the solemn sounds. They stopped at last, and the only noise was of distant traffic on the bypass.

We followed the edge of the industrial estate until we reached the main road. In spite of the barbed wire fence at the side, there was no gate or anything at the front. Anyone could walk or drive straight in, along a wide road designed for huge delivery trucks.

Different factory units had their own security gates, and some had CCTV cameras that rotated like searchlights. We weren't trying to get into any of the factories – we were heading for the car park by the old railway bridge. All the same, the cameras made me feel nervous.

"I hate that feeling of being watched," I muttered.

"I bet half these cameras are fakes," Dylan said. "And the other half, probably nobody's watching them. Anyway, what if they do see us? Like you said, we're not doing anything wrong."

Deeper into the estate, where some of the buildings looked as if they'd been empty for years, there were not so many cameras. Half the street lights were out. It was easy to slip from shadow to shadow, avoiding the light.

Once, a police car drove past slowly, and we froze in a shadow. But the car didn't stop. Soon after, we saw the glow of a torch ahead of us – probably a security man doing his rounds. We slid into the shadow of a rubbish skip, and when we looked out again, there was no sign of him.

Not much was moving – only the wind, blowing bits of rubbish here and there like dead leaves and a small creature that scuttled across the road and disappeared.

"Was that a rat?" I whispered.

"Probably. They say you're never more than 10 feet away from a rat these days. They're everywhere."

"Oh thanks, Dylan. That really makes me feel better."

We were coming towards the car park. It was empty, apart from a couple of abandoned vehicles. It was also very dark.

I began to wish we'd brought a torch with us. The only light was on my mobile, and it wasn't a very bright one. But I switched it on anyway. If there were more rats around, I wanted to see them.

We crossed the car park. Dylan wanted to be right next to the railway bridge, but I didn't. We sat down on a wall about half way along, with our backs to the river. I could hear the murmur of water in the darkness below.

I shivered, feeling the chill breath of the wind against my face.

"What do we do now?"

"We wait," said Dylan.

* * ★

We waited for a very long time. I switched my mobile off after a while to save the battery. The cold stones of the wall we sat on seemed to be freezing my bones.

The church clock chimed the quarter, then the half-hour. Half past midnight, and nothing had happened...

"This is a waste of time," I said. "Can we go back now?"

"Sssshh! I can hear something."

I listened.

"That's not a train. It's a van or something – diesel engine. Or maybe the ghost train is a diesel now, not a steam train? In another few years, it will be electrified. It could run along the Electric Mile."

Dylan didn't think this was funny.

A black van pulled into the car park. Its headlights swept over us, making me blink. It came to a stop near the bridge and just sat there. The lights were turned off, but nobody got out.

"Wonder what that van is doing here at this time of night," I said.

"Maybe the driver brought his girlfriend here. Nice romantic spot – car park on the industrial estate." Dylan made kissing noises in the darkness.

"Shut up a minute," I told him. "Can you hear anything?"

He grabbed my arm. He could hear it too.

Quietly at first, then louder, came the sound of a steam train. Its mournful whistle sounded once, then again.

We were hearing a train that didn't exist, on a railway line that had vanished years ago. This couldn't be happening! It just couldn't!

The noise got louder and louder. I wanted to run, but Dylan stopped me. He was still gripping my arm with the strength of terror.

There was nothing to be seen – just the sound of puffing steam and pounding pistons. Then it began to get quieter. I heard the whistle one more time. The sound died away into silence.

"There. You heard it," I said. I couldn't stop my voice from shaking. "Happy now?"

"Not as happy as I'll be when we get out of here." His voice wasn't too steady either.

We ran for it. Forget rats, forget police cars, forget everything – just get away.

Chapter 12:

In trouble

Things seemed more normal in Station Road. The lights were brighter, and there were a few cars going past. People came out of a pub, arguing among themselves.

We stopped running. But I could still feel my heart pounding away.

"Did that really happen?" I asked. "Or did we imagine it?"

"It happened all right. Wish I'd recorded it on my phone. That's what I meant to do, but at the time..."

"Yeah."

"That van we saw – I wonder if the driver heard the train," said Dylan.

"He must have. He was right by the bridge. The train must have, like, passed right through his van." The thought made me shiver.

Dylan said, "Maybe he didn't hear anything at all. Not everybody is sensitive to the paranormal."

Neither of us felt like going back to ask the driver. All we wanted was to go home.

The quickest way was through the town centre. It was Saturday night, and there were people about. We saw three Year 11 girls who looked as if they'd had a bit too much to drink. They were sitting in a bus shelter, waiting for a non-existent bus.

The blonde one nudged the red-haired one as we went past.

"Oh, come on," said her friend. "A bit young for you, Jess."

"Thass what I mean. Does their mummy know they're out?" And she giggled.

"Look out," said the third girl. "Here comes Jake Shipley. I bet he's on the scrounge again."

"Don't give him any money. He never pays it back."

Further up the road, we waited for the lights to change. I heard a scream and looked back. There was a fight going on at the bus shelter. The girls appeared to be struggling with Jake.

"Maybe we should call the police," I said.

"I think those girls can take care of themselves," Dylan said.

He was right. Screeching like monster-women from a horror movie, the girls were laying into Jake. They hit him, kicked him and pulled his hair. They got him on the ground, then stood looking down at him, admiring their handiwork. After that they walked off, laughing.

Slowly he picked himself up. He looked very angry.

"Let's get out of here," said Dylan. "Jake looks like he wants to kill somebody."

A moment later we heard an almighty crash. Jake had smashed the panel at the side of the bus shelter. Bits of shattered glass lay everywhere.

We hurried away. "That's going to make him even more paranoid," said Dylan.

"What's 'paranoid' mean, exactly?"

"He thinks people are out to get him. You know... following him, plotting against him, hating him. Thing is, he's right in a way – nobody likes him much. He doesn't hang around with Tom next door any more. He nicked fifty quid off Tom's mum and she banned him."

"Do you think things would be different if he'd never started smoking weed?" I asked.

"How would I know? Maybe he would have been like that anyway."

By now we were back in the quiet side-streets. There was no one about, and no traffic except...

"Oh-oh. Police car coming," said Dylan.

He pulled me into a gateway with a tall hedge that might hide us. Too late – we'd been seen. The car stopped and two coppers got out. One of them shone a light right in my face.

"Come out here where we can see you," he ordered.

They questioned us about where we'd been. We didn't mention the ghost train. We said we'd been hanging out in the town centre with some mates.

"And I don't suppose you were anywhere near the bus shelter," the policeman said in a weary-sounding voice.

"When it got smashed up, you mean?" I said. "Yeah, we saw the guy who did it. It was a boy from our school, in year 10 or 11. I don't know his name."

"He got beaten up by some girls and he was angry," Dylan put in.

"The girls are worse than the lads these days," the other policeman said.

They asked us where we lived, and how old we were.

"You're too young to be roaming around the town at this time of night," one of them said. "Do your parents know about it?"

"Er... no."

"Get in the car. We'll take you back home."

I'd often wondered what it would be like to ride in a police car. I thought it would be exciting to speed down the road, blue light flashing, siren wailing. But this was not an emergency. We drove quietly at normal speed, as if we were in a taxi or something.

Dylan was looking worried. "What are Vince and June going to say?" he muttered to me.

I hadn't thought of that. When we pulled up outside the house, I got a sick feeling in my stomach.

"Thanks for the lift. We can let ourselves in around the back," Dylan tried to say.

But the policemen got out of the car. "We'd like a word with your parents. Just so they know what's going on."

Dylan said, "They're not actually our parents..." It was too complicated to explain easily, and by this time, one of the coppers was ringing the front door bell. He had to ring two or three times. At last, Vince came to the door in his dressing-gown.

He looked horrified to see us on the doorstep with two policemen.

"Dylan! Luke! What's going on?"

★ ★ ★

We had pretty well ruined Vince's birthday weekend. He was very upset, and so was June.

They believed us, I think, when we explained what we'd been doing – nothing illegal. We hadn't been getting drunk, taking drugs or mugging old ladies. But what we had done, going out late at night on our own, was still wrong.

"Anything could have happened to you," said June. "*Anything.*"

"And the thing is, we're responsible for both of you," Vince said. "We're supposed to be looking after you, keeping you safe. How can we do that if you sneak out of the house in the middle of the night?"

"Sorry," I muttered.

Dylan said, "We won't do it again. I promise we won't."

"You certainly won't," said Vince. "There will be no more sleeping out in the base, for a start. And you're both grounded for a week."

June said, "How is your mum going to feel, Luke, when she knows about this?"

"Oh, please don't tell her!" I cried. "She's got enough to worry about already!"

In the end they decided not to tell Mum. "But if you ever do anything like this again," said Vince, "we'll have no choice. We will have to tell her. Do you understand?"

"Yes."

★ ★ ★

The next week passed very slowly. It was boring being grounded. We couldn't even go to the park at the end of the road. We couldn't kick a ball around in the back garden – it was too small. And I missed Saturday football practice.

The worst thing was the change in the atmosphere. June kept giving me sorrowful looks, as if she blamed me for leading Dylan astray. I wanted to tell her it was all his idea. But I knew that if I hadn't agreed to go with him, he would never have done it.

And Vince, who used to think I was good for Dylan because I got him to go out more, had changed his mind about me too. He retreated behind his newspaper and hardly spoke.

I tried to make up for what we'd done by being extra polite and helpful. But maybe it would never be the same as before. They probably wished they hadn't agreed to look after me. The trouble was, they were stuck with me now, until Mum came back. And that might not be for weeks.

Chapter 13:

The match

The following week I felt better. For one thing, the Easter holidays were getting close. For another, Amy was doing well on her new treatment; Mum said that if she carried on like this, they would come home soon after Easter. And then, like the icing on the cake, I got picked to play for the under-13s.

The only problem was that the match was in a town several miles away. I knew that for away games, people had to pester their parents for lifts, or arrange to share transport. But I didn't know if I could ask Vince for yet another lift.

"Go on, ask him," said Dylan. "I bet he won't mind. He'll tell you all about the football games he played when he was our age."

"You ask him," I said.

"Okay, I will. Where's the match?"

"Lowbury," I said, and he suddenly looked interested.

"I might come too, and cheer you on," he said.

In the end it was decided that we would all go, even June, although she definitely belonged to the non-football half of the population. Dylan had persuaded her to go along in case he got bored with watching the match. They could find something else to do, he said.

"Like sit down somewhere and have a nice cup of tea?" June said hopefully.

"Like look round the museum. There's quite a good museum in Lowbury."

"How do you know?" I asked him.

"I used to live near there."

"Dylan, you're weird," I said. "You're the only boy in the world who likes museums better than football."

★ ★ ★

It felt great to put on the red-and-black Mallenford strip for the first proper match I'd played in. I had been put in midfield. I desperately wanted to play well so that the coach would pick me again.

We knew that Lowbury would be hard to beat. Our team had lost the last three games against them. I saw that they had two players as tall as 15-year-olds, although the league was supposed to be for under-13s. But on our side we had a striker, Lemar, who was really good. If we could keep feeding the ball to him, Lemar would score goals all right.

The game started badly. Within the first five minutes, Lowbury had scored – and it was partly my fault. I didn't tackle one of the big forwards when I should have. He easily got past two of our defenders, who looked as nervous of him as I was.

"Come on, Mallenford!" I heard Vince yell from the touchline. "Don't be scared of them! They can't eat you!"

Maybe not, but they can break my legs, I wanted to say to him. *And when they do, I bet you won't volunteer as a substitute.*

I was a bit braver the next time the big guy thundered towards me. I tackled him, and to my surprise, I managed to get the ball off him. A quick series of passes reached Lemar, and he scored a brilliant equaliser.

By half-time the score was two-all. I felt I was doing all right. Nothing startling – not like my dreams of scoring a hat-trick and astounding everyone. But I hadn't made an idiot of myself. I had even helped to set up Lemar's second goal.

"You're doing great, lads," the coach told us. "Holding them to a draw would be a good result, but let's see if we can do better than that. Let's see if we can win this!"

When the second half started, Vince was still there to cheer for us, but June and Dylan had disappeared. It was what I'd expected. Watching an entire game would be too much for Dylan.

By now, the Lowbury players had realised that Lemar was our main threat. They were covering every move he made. But when he took a corner, they couldn't stop his beautifully aimed kick that curved across the goal-

mouth. Centre-forward Nathan headed it straight in…
3-2 to us!

Lowbury fought back hard – we had a couple of narrow escapes. Then our goalie sent out a long clearance that reached Lemar. He raced for the Lowbury goal, dodging one defender, then another. But the third one brought him down with a vicious-looking sliding tackle.

Lemar let out a cry of pain. He lay on the ground, clutching his ankle. The ref had already blown his whistle. He gave us a penalty, but Lemar couldn't take the penalty kick – he was being carried off the pitch. Nathan took it, and missed by a mile.

Without our best player, we hadn't a hope of staying in the game. In the end we lost 5-3. Even more depressing, Lemar had been taken to hospital to have his ankle X-rayed. If it was broken, he would be out of action for the rest of the season.

"That was so unfair," I said to Vince. "They knew Lemar was really good. They did it on purpose."

"That's how it looked to me, too," said Vince. But I could tell his mind was on something else. "I wonder where June and Dylan have got to? They've taken the car."

"I didn't know June could drive," I said.

"She doesn't do it very often. She only passed her test last year. I hope she's all right."

We waited for ages. The other players went away; soon we were the only people left on the pitch. Dylan wasn't answering his mobile, and Vince didn't want to ring June in case it distracted her from her driving. At last, he did ring her, but at that very moment we saw the car arriving. (Vince owned a car as well as his van – an ancient thing called a Ford Capri.)

The car stopped, rather jerkily. In the front bumper there was a big dent which hadn't been there earlier. June got out and let Vince get into the driving seat. I thought she looked upset. When Vince asked where she'd got to, she gave him a tell-you-later sort of look.

Dylan was very quiet on the way back. He didn't ask about the match, and I didn't tell him. It wasn't until the next day that I found out where he had been.

June sent Dylan down to the shop to get some milk, and while he was gone, she and Vince said they had something to tell me.

"Is it about Dylan's mum and dad?" I said. "He already told me what happened to them."

"I thought he might have done," said Vince. "It's on his mind a lot. Only natural really, but..."

June said, "Yesterday, he asked me to take him to where he used to live. He just wanted to look at the house, he said. So I thought, why not? It was only a couple of miles outside Lowbury. I didn't think there would be any harm in looking at his old house, although of course there are other people living there now. But that wasn't what he was really wanting to see."

She was looking upset again. Vince took up the story.

"He wanted to visit the place where the accident happened, but he didn't tell June that. They went round this corner, and suddenly he shouted STOP! and grabbed the steering wheel. He must have seen his mother do that on the day she was killed."

"I was so shocked, I lost control of the car," said June. "We hit a gatepost. If we'd been going faster, he could have killed us both."

Vince said, "Maybe that's what he wanted, at that moment … wanted to die, like his mother."

"He does do some dangerous things sometimes," I said, thinking of the level crossing. "And he wants to find out about ghosts and all that, because he would like to think that his mother's still out there somewhere. You know… that she didn't just vanish forever."

Vince said, "It's like he's got stuck in the past. It's all very well to grieve for someone, but if you keep on and on thinking about them, your grief never gets a chance to heal."

"If only he believed in God," June said with a sigh. "He needs to know the Father's love."

"What's the good of talking about the Father's love?" I said angrily. "Dylan hates all that. His own father wasn't exactly loving, was he? And mine wasn't, either. He left us when we needed him most."

Vince said, "But God isn't like that. He promised never to leave us or forsake us."

Nice words, I thought. Nice words, if they were true.

"If there is a God, and he loves us, why is the world in such a mess?" I asked.

"The world as it is now isn't how God meant it to be," said Vince. "The Bible says that things went wrong when people stopped listening to God and obeying him. God made us able to choose things for ourselves, see. And if we make the wrong choice... that's when bad things happen like when people break the rules of a football game and somebody gets hurt."

"God shouldn't have made the world like that, then," I said.

"Shouldn't have made us able to decide things? Are you sure?" said Vince. "Then we would be more like the plastic figures on a table-football game – unable to move unless somebody controls them."

"That wouldn't be much of a life," I said.

"No. But he gave us the power to choose, and if we want to, we can choose to follow him."

I would have liked to talk some more, but just then we heard Dylan coming back.

"So can you help us keep an eye on Dylan?" June said. "And tell us if he starts planning anything... well, anything dangerous?"

"I'll try," I said.

Chapter 14:
Listening

"There's a letter for you, Dylan," I called. Dylan took one glance at it, then dropped it on the doormat.

"Aren't you going to open it?" I asked him.

He shook his head. "I know who it's from."

"Your dad," I guessed. "So he can write to you from prison? What does he write about?"

"Don't know. I never open the letters."

The envelope lay on the doormat until the evening. Then I saw June pick it up, sighing to herself. She put it away in a cupboard with a bundle of other letters.

"Are they all from Dylan's dad?" I asked her. "Why do you keep them?"

"We hope that one day Dylan might want to read them. He might start to forgive his father."

"Why should he do that? I'm not surprised that he hates his dad, after what he did."

June said, "It's very bad for people to hold onto hatred. It's like a sickness, growing inside you, like…"

She stopped suddenly, looking embarrassed. I finished the sentence for her: "Like cancer, you mean."

"Yes. Even though you can't see it, it's destroying you on the inside. If Dylan could forgive his father, he could start to get on with his life. He could stop worrying about what's past and done with."

I thought this was funny coming from June. She didn't like Dylan worrying about the past, although she herself worried quite a bit about life in general.

"What will happen when his dad comes out of prison?" I asked. "Will Dylan have to go and live with him? Because I can tell you now, he won't want to."

"I don't know yet what will happen. I pray about it every day. It will be at least a year before his dad gets out – maybe things will have changed by then."

"Dylan will have changed, you mean? Don't count on it," I said.

★ ★ ★

Dylan, as he had promised, played football whenever I wanted to for a week, then said he never wanted to touch a football again. He helped me to mend my bike tyre so that we could go on another ride.

He was still interested in the ghost train. He seemed to have forgotten how terrified we felt when we heard it. I hadn't – and I was determined not to go on any more midnight expeditions.

"We could have another look at the tunnel, though," Dylan suggested. "In daylight. Nothing scary about that, is there?"

"What do you want to go there for?"

"To get some pictures of the tunnel and the bridge. Then I'll put them on that website – you know, where people post their ghostly experiences."

In the end I agreed to go with him. The Easter holidays had started and I needed something to do.

"We'd better take a chain so we can lock the bikes up," I said. "In case that guy Jake is there again."

"I heard Jake's done a runner," said Dylan. "Tom says he hasn't been at school for a week, and his mum's been round asking all his friends if they've seen him."

"What friends? I didn't think he had any."

"His ex-friends, then. The people he used to hang around with. But none of them know where he's gone."

"I bet his kid brother isn't crying too hard," I said.

We rode down the track to the old mill. Like the last time, it was deserted. But just to be on the safe side, we hid the bikes around the back of the ruined building, chained up to a rusting metal post.

Using his mobile, Dylan took some pictures of the railway bridge. Then we climbed up through the woods and went along the old railway line. He took some more pictures, complaining that they didn't look spooky enough. It was springtime, the sun was shining, and a few daffodils were growing under the trees.

"This looks more like 'favourite country walks' than 'paranormal experiences'," he muttered.

We came to the tunnel mouth. Dylan took some photos from different angles, and then he did something odd. He leaned against the padlocked door, with his ear right next to the wood.

"That's funny. I think I can hear a noise. Not a train noise," he said quickly. "Have a listen – see if I'm imagining it."

Rather nervously, I copied him, putting my ear to the door. But I couldn't hear anything, except bird noises in the woods and distant traffic on the industrial estate.

"You can't hear something like a motor running?" he said. "Quite a long way off, inside the tunnel?"

"No. But I can feel something – cold air around my feet. A wind is blowing into the tunnel, under the door."

The cold draught was passing through a small gap along the bottom of the door. It felt as if air was somehow being sucked into the tunnel, which was strange. Wasn't the tunnel blocked off at the other end?

Dylan said, "Long tunnels have outlets in the roof to help the air to stay clean. Ventilation shafts, I think they're called. If we go a bit further up the hill, we might find one."

He was off, climbing some rotting wooden steps in the side of the railway cutting. I followed him. I wasn't at all interested in the architecture of the tunnel, but I had told June I would try to keep an eye on Dylan.

After an uphill struggle through the woods, we came to what must be the top of a ventilation shaft. It looked like a huge, broad-based factory chimney, which the builders had started, but not finished. It was about as tall as a two-storey house. Trees had grown up around it, some of them so close that their branches hung over the top.

"I bet I could get up there," said Dylan. "I want to find out if I can hear that noise again."

The climb didn't look too dangerous. I'd seen him go up a much taller tree in the park when my football got stuck in the branches. He climbed this one easily. Then, sitting astride a broad branch, he inched himself towards the wall of the shaft.

"Don't lean over too far," I called to him. "The branch might break, and that shaft must be deep."

He laughed. "You're getting as bad as June."

Now he was level with the top of the wall. It looked very old, with the mortar between the bricks crumbling away. His foot hit a loose brick, and I heard it go plummeting down into the shaft.

"Dylan! Be careful!"

He wasn't listening. I saw him lean further over the wall.

"Dylan!" I yelled frantically.

It was as if he couldn't hear me. His whole attention was on what lay below him, deep down in the tunnel. He sat stone-still, listening hard.

Then he slid back along the branch and slithered down the trunk of the tree. His face was as pale as the moon.

"I heard a ghost," he said. "A ghostly voice coming up from the tunnel where all those people died."

"What?"

"It was calling for help. That's all it said, over and over. *Help… help… help me…* It must have been from one of the people who got trapped in the wreckage. Most of them died before they could be rescued."

Chapter 15:

A cup of cocoa

"How do you know it was a ghost?" I said. "Ghosts are supposed to appear after dark, aren't they?"

"It's always dark inside a tunnel."

I didn't like this thought. A ghost haunting the tunnel, day and night, year after year... trapped in unending darkness...

"What did it sound like?"

"Sort of hollow and echoing ... and desperate ... calling out for help that never came."

"Maybe it was a real person and not a ghost," I said.

"Don't be stupid. How would they have got in there? It was a ghost, all right. You'd know if you heard it – go on, climb up and listen."

"No way." Absolutely nothing would have made me climb that tree and lean out over the dark shaft.

"Okay, I'll see if I can record it on my phone."

He climbed up again, and I held my breath as he slid out along the branch. He listened intently. Then he used his mobile to take a short video.

On the ground, he played it back to me. We saw the inside of the shaft going down into darkness, its damp walls gleaming. And we heard... nothing at all.

"Are you sure you didn't imagine the voice?" I asked.

"Absolutely positive. But it wasn't very loud. This phone doesn't pick up quiet sounds too well."

Then he had a thought. "Of course, the fact that I couldn't record it... that's another proof that it really is a ghost."

I shivered. It was cold here in the shadow of the tall brick tower. It must be even colder down in the tunnel, far from daylight, far from anything living.

"Let's get out of here. I've had just about enough of this place," I said.

★ ★ ★

That night, something woke me – a door closing quietly, and the sound of footsteps on the stairs. I shot out of bed. Was Dylan trying to sneak out again?

But it was only June. She was in the kitchen, putting the kettle on, although the clock showed 2am. She said she often woke up in the middle of the night and couldn't get back to sleep.

"So I usually come down and make myself a nice cup of tea, and then I don't wake Vince with my restlessness. Would you like one? Or a cup of cocoa?"

I was wide awake by now, so I let her make me a cocoa. It was something I hadn't drunk for years, and it brought back memories of being about five years old, listening to a bedtime story. I used to love Thomas the Tank Engine and Bob the Builder. Really bad things just don't happen in that kind of book. I mean, nobody even gets hurt much, and absolutely no one ever dies.

That voice in the tunnel – that ghostly voice calling for help that never came – was still on my mind. Was that what it would be like to be dead? Trapped in darkness forever?

Or would it be like the heaven that Vince had talked about – no more death, no sorrow, no crying or pain?

"June," I said, "how can anybody really know what happens after you die? I mean, all that stuff in the Bible about living in God's house, seeing him face to face… Nobody can really know that's true, can they?"

"Why not?"

I thought that was a stupid question. "Because nobody's been dead and then come alive again."

"Somebody has," she said. "I mean Jesus. He died, and God brought him to life again. And he promised that anyone who believes in him will live forever."

"How can you be sure that's true?"

"I've known Jesus and followed him for a long time – since I was younger than you are now. And I know he keeps his promises. This is one of them: *Look! I stand at the door and knock. If you hear my voice and open the door, I will come in.*"

"I don't understand," I said. "What door does that mean?"

"It means your life. If you want to know Jesus, you can open the door of your life to him and let him in. One prayer – that's all it takes."

She made it sound so easy, I almost decided to do it. But then I drew back.

If God was real – if I could truly get to know him – he might want me to change. To be nice to people all the time. To tell the truth. To stop feeling angry about Amy. Would it be worth it?

I decided to step away from the door. Maybe one day I would open it... I'd think about it, anyway.

I drank my cocoa and went back to bed.

Chapter 16:

The rope

"I had this strange dream last night," Dylan said to me the next morning.

I said nothing. (Other people's dreams are about the most boring thing in the world, I always think.) But Dylan went on to tell me about it anyway.

"I dreamed I was trapped inside the tunnel," he said. "Not caught in a train crash – trapped in the blocked-up tunnel behind that locked door. And I had no food, and the only thing to drink was water that came in through the roof. And I had been there for days and days."

"Doesn't sound like a very exciting dream," I said.

"That's what was so weird. My dreams are usually much better than that – lots of crazy things going on. This one was just hours and hours of feeling cold and hungry and lonely and scared. It was horrible."

Even the memory of it made him shudder.

"And then I heard a noise. I thought there was someone up at the top of the ventilation shaft. I shouted for help, but nobody came. I shouted for ages…"

"Dylan," I said, "you know that voice you heard…are you absolutely sure it wasn't a real person?"

He looked uncertain. "I suppose it could have been. But I don't see how they could have got in there."

"They could have fallen down the shaft. Or maybe there's a way in at the other end. If there's even the faintest chance that anyone could be trapped in there, we have to do something!"

"Like what? Call 999? We'd have to tell them what we were doing. We'll get into trouble."

"They might not even believe us," I said. "You're the only one who heard the voice. Could you have imagined the whole thing?"

"No. I'm sure I heard *something*. I just don't know if it was a real person, or a ghost."

We looked at each other.

"We have to go back there and check," said Dylan. "No use getting into trouble for nothing."

"Maybe we should get Vince to come with us," I said. "If we do hear anything, he'll know what to do."

"No, don't tell him. I don't want to get him annoyed again."

"That's stupid, Dylan! He won't be annoyed if we help to save somebody's life."

"Okay, we'll tell him later. First of all, let's make sure there really is someone down there. Not a ghost, I mean. I don't want to get into trouble for the sake of somebody who's been dead for 100 years."

I told June we were going on a bike ride to the old mill. Half an hour later we were back at the ventilation shaft. Dylan had brought a back-pack with him, refusing to say what was in it. "Oh, just a couple of things that might come in useful," was all he would say.

He climbed up the tree and out along the branch. Once again he leaned over the wall, listening.

"Hey! Anybody there?" he shouted, and waited for a time. I could tell by his face that there was no answer.

Soon he came slithering back to ground level.

"I can't hear anything at all," he said, disappointed. "Why don't you try?"

I really didn't want to, but in the end he persuaded me to climb the tree. Very carefully – gripping the branch tightly in both hands – I inched my way towards the edge of the shaft. Then I looked down.

I'm not normally afraid of heights. But this was different. The shaft was so deep and so dark, I couldn't see the bottom. If I fell in, I would probably die instantly.

For a minute – long enough not to look like a total coward – I stared into the depths. I couldn't hear or see anything. But I could feel something… a draught of air, as if the tunnel was breathing.

And I could smell an odd smell that was somehow familiar. What was it?

"I'm coming back up," Dylan called. "I want to try something."

I climbed higher up the tree trunk so that Dylan could take my place on the overhanging branch. Then I saw that he had a coil of rope slung around his shoulders.

"Dylan! What are you doing?"

"I'm just going to let this rope down," he said.

"Are you totally mad?"

"Don't worry. I'm not going to do anything risky."

I didn't believe him. He had a set, determined look on his face. Knotting the end of the rope around the branch, he gave a sharp tug to test the strength of it. Then he let the coils of the rope drop down into the shaft. It didn't seem like a very strong rope. It was old, and not nearly as thick as the ropes we climbed up in PE lessons.

"That rope isn't safe," I said.

"It was the only one I could find." Lightly he swung the rope to and fro. I could hear it hitting the sides of the shaft.

If he climbed down there, he might not be able to get back up again. Or the rope might break. The darkness, the horrible darkness, would swallow him up.

"Dylan, you're not to go down there."

"Who says? How are you going to stop me?"

"I can't stop you. But if you start climbing down, I'll ring Vince and June." Holding onto a branch with one hand, I got my phone out. "I promised them I would let them know if you did anything dangerous."

"You did *what*?" He looked furious. "So now you're spying on me, are you?"

"I'm not spying. I just don't want to see you getting hurt. Or even killed."

"Why should you care if I get killed? Sometimes *I* don't care if I get killed."

"You're a friend. That's why."

He looked up sharply, as if he thought I was joking.

"I mean it," I said. "You're probably one of the best friends I've got... even if you do hate football."

He laughed then. Perhaps he was pleased with what I'd said. Anyway, he seemed to change his mind about going into the tunnel. He began to pull the rope up again. Then he stopped.

"The rope's got caught," he said, tugging it sharply. Suddenly he cried out and clutched the branch he was sitting on.

"What's the matter?"

He said, "Something pulled on the rope. Really hard. Nearly pulled me over."

He wasn't holding onto the rope any more. It was still knotted around the branch, but now it hung straight down into the shaft.

"You mean... there's somebody down there?"

"Somebody, yeah. Or *something*."

"Call down to them," I urged him.

"Is there anyone there?" His voice echoed in the depths of the shaft. No answer came.

And yet the rope was moving. It shivered like a tight bowstring, and pulled at the branch Dylan sat on.

"Something's climbing up the rope," he whispered. His face was white.

"What do you mean, something?"

"I don't know. A zombie, maybe. A dead thing. Something evil..."

Suddenly all the horror films I'd ever seen rushed back to my mind. Darkness, evil, fear – things that were dead and yet alive – rotting bodies that could still move...

This evil thing must have been shut up in the tunnel, but we had given it a way of escape. Soon it would be free.

I slithered down the tree, hardly noticing that I'd scraped all the skin off one hand. Dylan was close behind me.

We ran through the woods without looking back.

Chapter 17:
Something's not right

As we got closer to the old mill, I heard something – a voice calling through the trees.

"Dylan! Luke! Where are you?"

"That sounds like Vince," said Dylan.

Vince's white van was parked in the clearing. It was spattered with mud, and a broken branch was caught in the roof-rack. Then Vince himself appeared through the doorway of the ruin.

"Oh, there you are," he said. "Got a bit worried when I found your bikes, and no sign of you. Are you all right, lads?"

"Fine," said Dylan, although anybody could see this wasn't true. He was out of breath from running, and he still had a frightened look on his face. Probably I looked the same.

Vince said, "Something scared you did it, up in the woods?"

Before Dylan could deny it, I said, "We think there's a ghost in the old tunnel. Or maybe it's not a ghost..."

The whole story came spilling out. At the end of it, Vince looked grave.

"Why didn't you tell me about this earlier?"

"Because we thought we'd get into trouble."

"Well, never mind that now. Let's have a look at this ghost of yours." He went to his van and got out a powerful-looking torch. "Now then, take me to the place, and we'll see what there is to see. Maybe you just imagined it, Dylan."

"He didn't," I said. "I saw the rope move."

Dylan said, "Why did you come looking for us, Vince?"

"Because June was worried about you. She said she just felt something was wrong. Driving along that track – when I was lucky not to get stuck in all those potholes – I was telling myself it was a waste of time. But now I can see she was right to be worried. You're not safe on the loose, you two! Worse than I ever was at your age!"

He wasn't cross with us. He was smiling.

We went back up the hill. By now the sun was low, and long shadows stretched between the trees. Soon it would be dusk. If Vince hadn't been with us, I would never have dared to go back to the shaft entrance. But everything was less frightening when Vince was there.

He went up the tree as easily as if it was a ladder. Not bad for a man of his age, I thought. Then he shone his torch down the shaft, calling, "Hello? Anybody there?"

After a minute he shook his head. He pulled the rope up without any problem, untied the knot, and dropped it on the ground. Then he came back down the tree.

"Were you planning on climbing down that rope?" he asked us. His face was stern.

"I was," Dylan admitted. "But Luke persuaded me not to."

"Good for Luke. You could have killed yourself, Dylan! Or you could be lying at the bottom of that shaft with a broken leg!"

Suddenly I noticed something.

"The rope looks different from before. It wasn't frayed at the end like that."

"Yes, and there was more of it," said Dylan. "It was twice that length."

Oh-oh. That must mean…

"Then it looks like someone really did try to climb up," said Vince. "But the rope broke."

"So why didn't you see him lying at the bottom of the shaft?" I asked. "Why didn't he answer when you shouted?"

"Because it's not a real person!" Dylan cried. "It's something evil. Some kind of monster!"

"More likely it is a real person," Vince said. "He fell, but the fall didn't kill him. He could be in a bad way, though. We need to get help."

He took out his phone. Then he had a sudden thought. "Isn't there an easier way to get into the tunnel?"

"It's boarded up," I said. "And the door's locked."

"Show me."

We went down into the railway cutting, which was full of deepening shadows. Vince banged on the locked door and shouted. The noise sent birds flurrying out of the trees. But there was no answer from beyond the door.

"What should we do? Call 999?" I asked.

Vince was looking at the metal bars and the padlock that held the door shut. "I don't want to call emergency if there's no need to," he said. "We can soon get in here and find out. Dylan, can you run back to the van and fetch my screwdriver? The battery-powered one. Just inside the back door."

I could tell Dylan didn't want to go through the woods on his own. I went with him, and we took the torch. We needed it. By the time we returned to the cutting, it was nearly dark.

But where was Vince? Frantically, Dylan flashed the torch around, and then we saw him – lying on the ground at the mouth of the tunnel.

"Vince!" Dylan cried. "Are you all right?"

Vince got up, dusted himself down, and grinned at us. "Don't panic, lads. I was just having a look through that little chink under the door. Funny thing – I think I can see a bit of light inside."

I lay down and took a look. He was quite right. The tunnel wasn't completely dark inside. There was a narrow line of light, like a gap between window curtains. What on earth could be in there?

The power screwdriver whirred away. Vince was taking out all the screws that fixed the metal bars to the door. Without them, the padlock would be useless.

The last screw came out. The metal bar swung loose from the door. Vince got ready to push it open – then he stopped.

"There's something not right about all this," he said. "I wonder if I should call the police? Inside the tunnel, my phone won't be much good to me... no signal."

"What will you tell them, if you ring up?" I said.

"That's just it. I don't know."

Suddenly he came to a decision. "I'm going to go in and have a look around. You wait here, boys, and if I'm not out in five minutes, call the police. All right?"

"No. I want to come with you," said Dylan.

"Stay here," said Vince. "That's an order, Dylan. Do you hear me? I need you to keep watch. If anybody comes into sight, give a whistle to warn me."

He pushed the door, and it creaked open. Then he stepped into the darkness of the tunnel.

Chapter 18:

The secret of the tunnel

Now I could see that line of light more clearly. It was about a hundred yards inside the tunnel, running from roof height down to the ground. And I could hear the sound that Dylan had heard once before – the sound of a motor running. What was going on?

Forgetting that Vince had told us to keep watch outside, we gazed after him. Vince crept quietly towards the light. He lifted what seemed to be the edge of a curtain and went through the gap. For an instant I caught a glimpse of bright lights and green leaves, like a ferny jungle growing inside the tunnel. Then the gap closed again.

I held my breath. Wait five minutes, then call the police, he had told us.

But after only a minute, he appeared again. He came hurrying back to us.

"You'll never guess what this is! I believe it's a cannabis farm. You know – like on that TV programme. Only instead of a house, it's in a tunnel!"

"Is there anybody in there?" Dylan asked.

"No. It probably doesn't need much looking after. There's a generator to power the lights and heaters. I suppose whoever set it up comes back now and then to check on it, and refuel the generator, and harvest the plants when they're ready. Very clever."

"The owners might come back anytime," I said nervously.

"Yes. I'd better call the police," said Vince.

He walked away from the tunnel mouth until he could get a signal on his phone. Then he had a long conversation. I heard part of it.

"In the old railway tunnel under Mar Hill... A cannabis farm, just like on the telly... Yes, I'm absolutely certain... Vincent Robertson, 11 Valley Road, Mallenford... No, actually it was two young lads who got onto it..."

I looked around for Dylan. Suddenly, I realised he'd disappeared. And there was only one place he could have gone – into the tunnel.

Vince had told us to stay outside. But he had his back to me; he was still talking on his phone. I slipped inside the door. Dylan was heading for the gap in the curtain. He was easy to spot – he was using Vince's torch.

"Dylan! Come back, you idiot!"

Dylan said, "I just want to have a look, that's all."

Actually, I felt the same. I wanted to see this strange place. And it would only take a minute.

My feet splashed through puddles on the floor. Cold drops of water fell on my head. The tunnel was a chilly, dark place – until you went between the curtains.

There, suddenly, it was full of light and warmth. Bright lights shone down on the growing plants. Heaters warmed the air, and there were more curtains at the far end to keep the heat in.

The cannabis plants were growing in long metal troughs. They were about two feet tall, green and leafy. They seemed to be doing well in this unnatural environment, where no sun shone and no wind blew, and the only sound was the purr of the generator.

"I wonder how much this lot is worth," Dylan said, wandering along the rows of plants.

"When it's all cut down, there will be tons of the stuff," I said. "How do they get it out of here without being seen?"

Suddenly Dylan froze.

"Look," he whispered, pointing into a corner.

I went closer to see what he'd found. Big bags of fertiliser, a metal tank, a hosepipe... What was so amazing about that?

Then I saw it. There was someone lying there, on a sort of bed made of fertiliser bags. He lay very still. His eyes were closed.

"Is he dead?" I gasped.

"No, he's still breathing," Dylan muttered. "It's Jake Shipley. Remember I said he'd disappeared? I bet he was here all the time."

"Do you think all this belongs to him?"

"No way. How would Jake set all this up?"

There was a shout from behind us. Vince's voice echoed along the tunnel. "Come out, lads! I've been told to fasten up the door and leave it like we found it."

Jake's eyelids flickered. He stirred, and groaned, and began to wake up.

"He was shut in here," I said. "Like a prisoner. What's going on?"

"Maybe it was him that I heard calling for help," said Dylan. "He was the ghost."

Jake rubbed his eyes. He looked rough, I thought. His face was gaunt, and there were dark shadows under his eyes.

"Who are you?" he said, staring at us. "How'd you get in here?"

"Through the door at the end of the tunnel," said Dylan. "It's open now. You can get out if you want to."

"Better hurry, though," I said. "It's going to be locked again."

At once Jake tried to get up. But he stumbled, moaning in pain. He couldn't seem to put much weight on his left foot.

"Want a hand?" I offered.

"Don't touch me!" Jake hissed. "Leave me alone!"

He began limping between the rows of plants. We followed him, full of curiosity.

"What were you doing here, Jake?" Dylan asked him.

He stopped. "How do you know my name?"

"I live next door to your mate, Tom. Did you know your mum's dead worried about you? She thinks you've done a runner."

Jake swore. "How long have I been in here? Feels like years."

"It must be at least a week," said Dylan. "That's when your mum started asking if anyone had seen you."

"How did you get shut in here?" I asked him.

At first I thought he wasn't going to answer. Then he muttered, "I heard the train. That's what started it. People say it's unlucky... They're right."

"You mean the ghost train?" said Dylan.

"Yeah. I'm at the mill and I hear the train. And then I look up, and I see something on the bridge."

He started moving again, limping painfully towards the tunnel entrance. It was very dark on the far side of the curtains. Dylan shone the torch on the ground to light our path.

Dylan said, "You actually saw the ghost train?"

"No. It's dark, but I know what I'm seeing. Not a train – it's a van, a black van with no lights on. Driving across the railway bridge."

"That's impossible," I said. "There are gates at the far end, locked gates. How could a van get onto the bridge?"

"Never mind that," Dylan said impatiently. "What happened?"

"I follow it. I get up onto the railway line. And the van's parked up, empty, and there's like a door open into the tunnel. So I go in."

"Why?" I gasped. "All on your own in the dark? Why did you do it?"

"I was told to. I had orders. These people are dangerous, that's what I was told. You have got to stop them, Jake."

He was starting to sound quite mad, like before, when he talked about having a chip planted in his brain. But then, anyone might sound crazy after being locked up for a week alone without food.

"So I went in, and then I heard people coming – two of them. I hid in there." He pointed to the side of the tunnel. Dylan flashed the torch in that direction, showing a sort of alcove in the wall.

"They didn't see you?"

"No, they went out and shut the door. And I heard the van drive away. And then I found out I was trapped."

"It must have been terrible," I said.

Dylan said, "I bet you were pleased to find all that weed, though."

Jake swore again. "It's not ready to use. And I'm starving. I'd swop the lot for a pizza."

"Hurry up, lads!" Vince shouted from the door. "Or do you want to be locked in?"

Jake stopped dead. "Who's that?" he said.

"It's all right," I said quickly. "He wouldn't really lock us in."

"He better not try. If he does, I'll kill him." Jake's voice was savage.

Dylan said, "We came here to help you, you know. It was us that let down that rope."

"What? You tricked me! You let me start climbing up and then you cut the rope!"

"No, no. The rope broke," I said.

"I knew it was just a trick! I knew they'd never let me out of here! I fell down. I could have broken my ankle!"

"Jake, it was an accident," said Dylan. "We didn't mean to hurt anybody."

I said, "Come with us. The door's open. You can get out right now."

"You're on their side! You're trying to trick me again! I'll get you for this!"

He swung around. Something glittered in the torchlight.

"Look out!" I yelled. "He's got a knife!"

Jake lunged towards us. I dived to one side. But Dylan wasn't quick enough. He screamed in agony as the knife cut into him.

The torch dropped to the ground – everything went dark. I couldn't see where the door was. My ears were filled with Dylan's screams and Jake's crazy shouting.

"I'll get you for this! I'll kill you!"

Chapter 19:
The knife

"Stop it! Stop it right now!"

Vince was shouting even louder than Jake. The sound told me which direction I should take, and I crept towards the door.

I heard Vince go past me, towards the other two. "Watch out," I said. "Jake's crazy and he's got a knife."

"I said stop it! Put the knife down!"

Vince's voice was strong, full of authority. Dylan stopped screaming. Even Jake was quiet for a minute.

"I'm not going to hurt you, lad," Vince said. He sounded unbelievably calm. "Look, the door's just there. You can get out. No one's stopping you."

"Trying to... trick me again... " Jake gasped.

"No. No tricks. The door's open. Look, I'll show you."

He switched on a small light, probably on his phone. Dangerous, I thought. It would make him a target – Jake could see where he was.

I crouched down as the thin beam of light picked out the doorway. It was only a few feet away from me now. I could get out, and Jake would be too slow-moving to catch me.

But Vince was going further into the tunnel. Closer to Jake and his knife.

Oh God, help! Help us! It was a silent scream, not a prayer.

"Look, son, there's nothing to be scared of," Vince said, still in that calm voice. He shone the light on his own face. "An old man and a couple of kids. That's all. We can't possibly hurt you."

"Get away from me! Don't touch me!"

"All right. I'm not coming near you. I just want to make sure Dylan's okay."

I heard Dylan moaning in pain. At least that meant he was still alive. Then Vince's light showed him lying on the ground, his hands pressed to his side.

"It's all right, Dylan, lad. It's all right," said Vince.

But it wasn't all right. There was blood on Dylan's hands. Would he bleed to death here in the tunnel?

"I need to get him to a doctor," Vince said. "I'm going to pick him up. Hold my phone for me, will you?"

He was talking to Jake. Amazingly, Jake did as he was asked. He held the light while Vince, grunting with the effort, picked Dylan up in a fireman's hold.

"Go on; you go first," Vince said to Jake, as if they were queuing for a lift or something.

Jake's lurching footsteps came closer. He was still holding the phone in a hand that shook. The wavering beam lit up the doorway again.

I wanted to run out of the door – but something told me to stay quite still. If I startled Jake, anything might happen. It was the hardest thing I'd ever done, lying there with my face to the ground, as those limping feet went past me and out of the tunnel.

What would he do now? Try to lock us in?

But he didn't. As I scrambled to my feet and followed Vince out of the door, Jake was just standing there. Instead of the dark, dripping tunnel roof, the starlit sky arched over him. Jake gazed upwards as if he couldn't quite believe it.

The danger wasn't over yet – he still had the knife. He might still do something crazy, if he heard those voices in his head.

But there wasn't time to worry about that. We had to get Dylan to the hospital right away. He was moaning in agony, and Vince's jacket was dark with blood.

"Call an ambulance," Vince gasped. It was taking all his strength to carry Dylan.

"Where should I tell them to come to? We'll never get Dylan back to the van."

"Then we'll take him over the bridge. Tell them… the industrial estate, the railway bridge."

"But there's a gate at the far end."

"Call the fire brigade too. They'll have metal-cutters. Hurry!"

I felt in my pocket for my phone. Oh, no... it wasn't there. It must have fallen out somewhere in the woods or inside the tunnel.

Jake was still holding Vince's phone in one hand. The other hand held the knife. Would he give me the phone? Or would he still think I was an enemy trying to trick him?

Oh, God... I don't know what to do... help me!

Be brave, Luke. Just ask him for the phone.

What? Jake wasn't the only one who heard voices in his head. Where had that come from?

Go on, just ask him.

"Jake," I said timidly, "can I have that phone, please?"

"Oh." Jake looked surprised, as if he'd forgotten he still had it. He held out his hand. "Here you are. I'm off now. See you."

And he began to walk unsteadily away. He looked like he needed a doctor too, but I didn't want to risk making him angry again. I rang 999. As I was explaining where the ambulance should come to, Jake vanished into the dark forest.

"The Mallenford industrial estate?" said the voice at the end of the phone. "Can you give me more details, please?"

"Tell them to go to the car park near the old railway bridge."

"I'm sorry, could you repeat that? My map isn't showing a railway bridge."

My thoughts raced. How could I describe the place? What if they got it wrong? Every second might count.

Ice cream vans came to mind, a memory from weeks ago. Ice cream vans hibernating in winter. "It's the car park opposite the ice cream place," I said. "Oh, tell them to hurry… please…"

Vince, breathing heavily, was carrying Dylan along the path of the old railway. He had to keep stopping to rest. He was strong, but Dylan's body hung down like a dead weight.

The moaning had stopped. Was Dylan unconscious? He'd lost a lot of blood. Was he still alive?

"Call June," Vince said through gritted teeth. He had no spare energy for talking. "Number's on my phone."

I rang her and gabbled out the story. I expected her to panic, but now that the worst was happening, she didn't fall apart. She said she was getting in the car, and I told her where to go.

We reached the bridge. Vince had to stop again, leaning his weight on the stone parapet. He looked completely drained. I knew he couldn't go much further.

I could see the gates at the far end of the bridge. I was hoping to see an ambulance and a fire truck, but the car park was empty.

Vince staggered on. And now I could hear a distant sound, the sound I was longing for – the wail of an emergency vehicle.

"Run to the gate," Vince said hoarsely. "Wave to them."

Oh God, please… don't let it be too late…

Chapter 20:

Emergency

The car park, which had been empty and dark, was suddenly full of flashing lights. I saw an ambulance, a fire truck and a police car. From beyond the gates at the end of the bridge, I shouted and waved frantically.

"Over here! My friend – he's been stabbed. Oh, hurry up!"

By the time Vince got to me, the firefighters were cutting through the chain that held the gates shut. It fell free with a clang. The gates creaked open, and the two paramedics took Dylan from Vince's arms. They laid him on a trolley and lifted him into the ambulance. A minute later they were speeding out of the car park.

The police wanted to question us. Who had stabbed Dylan? Where was he now, and was he still armed?

I told them Jake's name. Vince said he was probably hiding in the woods somewhere. "But be careful if you go near him. He's been shut inside the old tunnel for several days, and he's not thinking clearly."

"He's crazy, you mean," I said. "And he still has his knife."

Soon June arrived in the car. Vince asked the police if we could go now. He was desperate to get to the hospital and see how Dylan was.

"All right, but we'll need you to make a statement later on. Is the boy a relative of yours?"

"We're his foster parents."

"But he's like a son to us," said June.

Vince, normally a law-abiding driver, forgot about speed limits as we raced to the hospital. We were told that Dylan was having emergency surgery. There was nothing we could do, except wait.

"And pray," said June.

I knew she would say that. We could pray, but was anyone listening? Back at the tunnel, I thought I had heard God speak to me. But now, under the bright lights of the hospital, I wasn't so sure. Maybe I had imagined it.

Vince and June believed in God, a God who loved everyone like a father. What if they were wrong, though? Perhaps there was no father-God. Perhaps there were no gods at all – only people struggling to survive in a world full of pain and fear.

And when they couldn't survive any longer... what then? Did they just vanish into the darkness?

* * *

I hate hospitals. You feel trapped inside a huge machine which whirrs and beeps endlessly, not caring who you are or why you're there. Hurrying footsteps echo along the corridors. Distant voices speak a strange language full of meaningless medical words.

We waited for hours. I must have fallen asleep; I woke up to find I was leaning against June's shoulder. She was wide awake, and Vince was pacing up and down, up and down.

It was true what June had said. Dylan was like a son to them – they loved him as much as any father or mother could have done. Vince had even risked his life to rescue Dylan.

Did Dylan love him in return, though? I wasn't at all sure. Dylan was such a secretive person, hardly ever showing what he felt.

At last we got some news. A tired-looking doctor told us that Dylan had come through the operation all right, although his spleen had to be removed. (Another of those strange words. What was a spleen?) He was now in intensive care.

"So he's going to be OK?" June said.

"Well… we hope so. The next 24 hours will be crucial."

Translated from medical speech, this meant: *we don't know*.

June stayed at the hospital, so as to be there when Dylan came round from the anaesthetic. She told Vince and me to go home. We were both so weary that we didn't argue.

I fell into bed and slept for hours. When I woke up, I couldn't understand why I was in bed, fully dressed, at 4pm. Then I remembered.

The house was full of silence. The car had gone from the drive. Had Vince heard some news and gone rushing back to the hospital?

There was a list of phone numbers on the wall. I tried calling Dylan's phone, but it was switched off. Vince's phone was still in my pocket, and June didn't possess a mobile. I could only wait, with a sick feeling in my stomach.

The house phone rang, and I snatched it up. But it wasn't from the hospital – at least, not the local one. It was Mum.

"Guess what? They say Amy is doing well enough to go home! She'll have to keep on taking the medicine, and go back for a check-up in three months. But they're really pleased with her progress! So we'll be home in a few days, if I can get the flights."

Mum sounded extremely happy. I tried to feel happy too, but it was difficult. After a minute she noticed.

"Is something the matter, Luke? Are you all right?"

"I am, but Dylan isn't. He's in hospital. He got stabbed."

"He got *what*? Did you say stabbed?"

I should have kept my big mouth shut. She was horrified, and she wanted to know every detail of what had happened. The phone call must be costing an arm and a leg.

"Are you sure you're OK, Luke? What were Dylan's parents thinking about, letting you get into danger?"

"It wasn't Vince's fault – he told us not to go into the tunnel, but we didn't listen. And then he came in and rescued us. He saved Dylan's life."

In a way, I rather enjoyed all the fuss – at least Mum was worrying about me for a change. But I wished she would ring off, in case anyone else was trying to get through.

Suddenly I heard a key in the door.

"Got to go now, Mum. See you soon."

It was June who came in. Vince had gone to the hospital so that she could come back and rest. She looked shattered.

She said, "Dylan's not doing too badly. 'In a stable condition' is what they said. But he's not out of the woods yet. You know, they had to give him more than 20 pints of blood during the operation."

I made her a cup of tea, and she drank it gratefully. She said she wasn't hungry.

"I'll get washed and changed, and then I'm going to church," she said. "Want to come with me?"

"Church? It's not Sunday today, is it?"

"No, it's Good Friday."

Good Friday? What was so good about it?

But I went along with her. She said that Dylan still needed our prayers.

Chapter 21:

Changes

I thought the church service might take my mind off Dylan. But it didn't, because it was all about death – the death of Jesus, who was tortured and killed in Jerusalem, two thousand years ago.

We watched part of a video retelling the story. Being crucified was a slow, cruel, dreadful way to die. I couldn't understand why Jesus had to go through it. If you believed the Bible, he was God's Son and he could do miracles. Why couldn't he stop his enemies from killing him?

To my surprise, the preacher started talking about this.

"Jesus was born on earth, and lived and died here, for a reason. He was on a mission, and his number one aim was to show people what God is like – to show them God's love.

"He could have avoided being captured by his enemies. When he went to Jerusalem, he knew he was going to his death; he told his friends about it beforehand. He was dreading it.

"And yet he still went, because he knew that by dying, he could save us. He would bear the punishment

134

for all the wrong in the world, all the things that take people away from God – all the hatred, lies, violence, envy, anger... He died so that we can live. He went down into darkness so that we can walk in the light."

Suddenly I thought of Vince going into the tunnel, alone and unarmed. He'd heard Dylan screaming. He knew there was great danger, but he still went in – all because of Dylan.

"The life and death of Jesus show us that God loves us. And we have a choice to make. We can turn towards him, and give our lives to him, and walk in the light. Or we can turn away from him, into the darkness.

"If you've never made that choice, never opened the door to God's love, then you can do it now. It's so simple. Just pray this prayer along with me: *Lord, I'm sorry for the times when I've messed up. Thank you for giving up your life to save me. I want to know you and follow you.*"

Inside my head, I echoed his words. I wasn't 100 per cent sure that God was real – but if he was, I wanted to know him. I wanted to walk in the light, not the darkness.

Then I added some words to the prayer. *And please help Dylan to get better...*

★ ★ ★

Dylan was a lot better by the next day. He'd been moved out of intensive care to an ordinary ward, where he could have more visitors. Vince took me to see him in the afternoon.

He still had tubes going into his arm. He was lying quite still because it hurt his stomach when he moved. "I've got a scar from here to here," he said, quite proud of the fact. "And they took my spleen out. Whatever that means."

I had been looking it up on the Internet. "The spleen is near the liver. It helps to get rid of bacteria and old blood cells. You can survive without it – lucky for you."

"Yes, but what about my football career?" said Dylan. "Will I ever be able to play again, doctor? I hope the answer's no."

Then he asked if we knew what had happened to Jake.

"The police are looking for him," said Vince, "but they haven't found him yet."

"He broke into Vince's van, though," I said. "At least we think it was him."

That morning, when Vince went back to the mill to get his van, he'd found the side window smashed in. He was worried that his tools might have got nicked, but all that had been taken was his lunchbox, containing an apple and a stale cheese sandwich.

Nobody knew where Jake was. He hadn't gone back home – he was probably afraid of getting arrested if he did. Maybe he had really done a runner this time. Except that he couldn't run... he could hardly walk.

"He should go to hospital and get that foot looked at," said Vince. "If he's broken a bone, it needs to be set right, or he might end up limping for the rest of his life."

"Good," said Dylan. "He deserves it, after what he did to me."

"The lad wasn't in his right mind. You mustn't blame him too much," said Vince.

"Yes, and I bet he's still crazy now. He'll stab somebody else if they don't catch him," said Dylan.

Vince told Dylan the next part of the story. From the mill, he had gone up to the tunnel mouth, looking for his power screwdriver. Someone – the police, most likely – had been there before him. The metal bars had been screwed back into place, locking the door as before, and his screwdriver had gone. (But he did find my phone in the undergrowth, by ringing the number. I was very pleased to get it back.)

At the police station, where Vince and I had to make a statement about the stabbing, he asked about his screwdriver. He was told he couldn't have it back just yet. It might be needed as evidence in the case.

"The only fingerprints you'll find on it are mine," said Vince, looking worried. "You surely don't think it was me growing all that cannabis stuff?"

"It wasn't Vince," I said. "It was two guys in a black van. Jake saw them driving over the railway bridge." I told them everything that Jake had said.

"So it's the car park and the railway bridge that you should be keeping an eye on," I said. "Those men will have to come back sometime to get the weed."

Vince said, "You'll need to replace the lock and chain on those gates, or they'll know somebody's been in."

"I wonder how the men managed to get a key for that," I said.

"Most likely they cut through an old padlock chain, and put their own one on," said Vince. "Same thing at the tunnel. They broke in – you could see where the door had been damaged – and then fitted new bars and locks."

The policeman gave us a suspicious look. "You seem remarkably well-informed about all this," he said. At first I thought he was being serious, but then he grinned at me.

"If we catch the guy who stabbed your friend, do you think you could identify him?" he asked.

"Sure," I said.

"Then you might be hearing from us again."

But several days went by without any news.

In the meantime, Dylan came out of hospital. He was told to take things easy – no sports and no bike rides for several weeks. He got straight onto his computer and started posting his photos of the tunnel on the paranormal website.

"But Dylan, you didn't hear a ghost in the tunnel," I said. "That voice shouting for help was probably Jake."

"How do you know? And anyway, what about the ghost train? We both heard it. I wish I'd managed to record it."

I thought of what the preacher had said once in church. "Some people say they can't believe in God because there's no proof that he exists. But they find it easy to believe in a whole lot of other unproved ideas – ghosts and fortune-telling and aliens and magic. They'd rather believe in that kind of thing than in God. Because when you do put your trust in him, he starts to change your life."

Was my life going to change? Actually, I had already noticed a difference – I didn't feel so scared of dying. I knew that when my time came to die, I wouldn't go down into darkness. I would walk in the light of God, and see his face.

★ ★ ★

Two days later, Mum and Amy came back. Dad picked me up and took me to the airport to meet them.

I was sort of expecting that Amy would still be in a wheelchair, like she was when they left. I was amazed to see her walking into Arrivals on her own two feet. She even had hair! (Not very long hair – it was shorter than mine – but it looked much better than total baldness.)

Dad gave her an enormous hug. When he let go of her, there were tears in his eyes... tears of happiness. I felt a stab of envy, sharp as a knife. I knew that whatever

I did, even if I captained the England team, I would never make Dad feel as happy as he was at that moment. And what had Amy done? Been ill and got better – that was all.

And she might not be completely well. The cancer might come back, like it did before. We would just have to wait and see.

Amy moved her things back upstairs – she could climb stairs all right now. Our living room became a proper room, not a hospital ward. And I moved back home from Dylan's house.

It felt good to be home. Things were more the way they used to be before Amy got ill. She was like a normal sister, not an invalid. We had long arguments over stupid little things, such as who got the best seat on the sofa.

"Mum! It's not fair! He sat there last time."

"Only for five minutes. That doesn't count," I said, not moving an inch.

She punched me, and I looked at her, amazed.

"What's the matter?" she said.

"That is the first time you've hit me for months and months. Go on, do it again, I won't mind a bit."

"Come back and see us anytime you like," said June, when I collected the last of my things – my bike, my backpack and my football.

"We're really going to miss you, lad," said Vince.

"And I'll miss you all," I said. "Thanks for letting me stay here."

Dylan said, "Call me whenever you want to play football."

"Oh yeah... and you'll tell me the doctor won't let you play. I know you, Dylan."

The letterbox rattled. It was the local free paper being delivered. I glanced down at it and saw the headline.

"Hey! Look at this!"

CANNABIS IN HAUNTED TUNNEL

Mallenford police, on Monday, arrested two men suspected of growing a large crop of cannabis in a deserted railway tunnel.

"It was a well-organised setup," a police spokesman said. "There was artificial light and heating, like in a plant nursery. It would never have been detected by our infra-red cameras because it was deep underground."

The cannabis growers are believed to have reached the tunnel by way of a bridge and an abandoned railway line. According to local people, the line is haunted – it was the scene of the Mar Hill Railway Disaster in 1869. Several people claim to have heard the sound of a ghostly steam train late at night.

Following a tip-off, police kept the railway bridge under surveillance. They arrested two men who arrived at midnight and tried to drive a van across the bridge. Interestingly, the van contained a powerful sound system with a recording of steam train noises. It appears that the men were keeping up the "haunted" reputation of the railway line so that no one would come near it.

Two men were remanded in custody. The cannabis plants were removed and destroyed.

"Well, I never!" said Vince.

"I told you there's no such thing as ghosts," said June.

"That is so dumb," said Dylan. He looked disappointed. "I thought the ghost train was for real. And now I find out it's like every single episode of that stupid *Scooby-doo* cartoon."

Then he brightened up. "Hey, there's something I saw on the Internet. A ghost's been seen at Mallenford Hall. There's an actual photo on the website – a face at an attic window, in a room that's been locked up for years."

"And I suppose you want to investigate it," I said.

"Yes – as soon as I'm well enough. You can come too, if you want."

"No thanks," I said. "I've heard enough about ghosts to last me for the rest of my life."